Intervene
Guy Lane

Chapters

Water Landing

Upstream from the popular camping site in the Alligator Creek National Park is a wide, flat boulder that offers a dramatic view of the forested hillside across the valley and the fast-flowing creek. Humidity tinges the warm air at the end of the tropical wet season. An overnight downpour has set the stream in flood, and the roar of moving water fills the air like TV white noise.

The sky is deep blue, and a cloud drifts slowly, its shadow racing across the landscape. As the cloud moves, an extraordinary sight becomes visible; a halo surrounds the sun forming a perfect circle. A jetliner crosses the sky, leaving a bright contrail that slices the halo into two equal parts.

From the forest, walk two young men. Toddy and Al are barefoot, dressed in jeans and t-shirts. Toddy has a stocky build and a shock of black, curly hair. Al is smaller, and wiry, with pale skin and freckles. He has a yellow cotton satchel slung over his shoulder. The two young men step onto the boulder, their regular spot in the sun.

"Check that out," says Al, looking up at the sun.

"Have you got the rollies?" asks Toddy.

"That's caused by ice crystals in the stratosphere."

"Don't tell me we left the fags in the house." Toddy starts patting himself, searching for the cigarettes. "Where are they?" he asks, annoyed.

"That's a portent for something," says Al, in awe of the halo and contrail.

"It's important not to forget the bloody smokes."

"Check behind your ear."

"*Ahhh*. There they are." Toddy grips the rolled cigarettes

1

between his lips and searches his jeans for a means to light them. First, he tries the left pocket, then the right. Then he loses track of which pocket he's checked.

"You're such a doofus," Al retrieves a box of matches from his bag, strikes a match and leans towards his mate, sheltering the flame with his cupped hand.

"I'm not a doofus," Toddy tells him. "I'm just relaxed."

With both cigarettes pinned between his lips, Toddy pushes the tip into the flame and puffs repeatedly until bright orange embers illuminate the ends. Al shakes out the match and places the burnt stump into its box, and the box in his bag.

Toddy draws on the cigarettes and then passes one to his mate. Al takes a drag on the cigarette. He holds the smoke in for a second, and then, simultaneously the two young men exhale a cloud of pale blue smoke. The smoke races forward, intermingling, and fading.

As Toddy and Al watch the smoke dissipate, their attention is caught by a disturbance up ahead of them, about ten meters away. At first, it is barely noticeable, but then they see a hazy, amorphous shape forming above the creek.

They glance at each other, confirming that they have both observed the same thing. The shape takes on the form of a cluster of pearlescent blue spheres, glistening like soap bubbles. As Toddy and Al watch, the bubbles multiply in number.

"Do you see that?" asks Al, dumbfounded.

Toddy looks nervously to his mate, "Blue bubbles. Is that what you're seeing?"

"That's exactly what I'm seeing."

The blue bubbles become opaque with flickers of light

appearing between them. A hissing noise comes from within. The bubble cloud grows to the size of a Kombi Van. The sound rises in intensity, like a wild animal hissing or a pressure vessel leaking air. A loud CRACKLE startles the two young men, and they jump to their feet.

Then, an ear-splitting CRACK!

The bubbles disappear in a flash of light. In their place, *a man pops into existence.* He seems to hang in the air for a few seconds - naked and clutching a brightly coloured object to his chest - then he plummets into Alligator Creek and disappears under the foaming white water.

The object floats to the surface, flashing and pulsating with iridescent colours like the skin of a dying tuna. The object flows downstream, between the boulders.

The man comes to the surface, face down and motionless. The current takes him away, too.

Toddy and Al watch, stunned, as the body drifts into a narrowing between the rocks and disappears into the rush of white water.

"Quick," shouts Al, scrambling down the boulders towards the body as it tumbles down the waterfall.

Toddy races ahead, lunges and catches hold of the man's wrist. "I've got him," he shouts.

The two young men struggle to hold onto the hand, but the force of the white water is too much, and the fallen man slips from their grasp.

"Quick!" They leap from one boulder to the next as the body rolls down the rapids, bouncing from rock to solid rock. Up ahead is a roar of white water where the creek falls into a deep hole. Al leaps ahead and wedges himself between two rocks and lashes out. He manages to get his hand on the big man's ankle, but his grip only holds for a few seconds. Toddy leans in and grabs a wrist. Between them, they arrest the big man's journey.

"Don't let him go!"

Struggling against the dead weight, Toddy and Al haul the man from the creek. They get his head and upper body free of the water. It's not clear whether he is alive or dead. He's a big bloke, heavy and muscular, like a cage wrestler. It is all they can do to drag him out of the water and onto a pebble beach, away from the fast-running creek.

"Turn him over," says Toddy. They clutch the naked man by the arms and haul him onto his back then step back in astonishment. The man is six-foot-four, with six-pack muscles on his belly. His biceps are as thick as legs of lamb. His hair is cropped short in a crew cut.

"Is he dead?" asks Al, catching his breath.

The man writhes slowly, his face streaming with blood from a wound on his brow. He has grazes and cuts on his shoulders and legs. His movements become more pronounced. Then his eyes flicker open. He appears startled to see the sky. His face distorts into an expression of abject astonishment, and he sits upright.

Next, he retches up a bit of the creek. He leans forward, gagging and spitting to clear his airways. Blood drips from his face and the red spreads across the wet pebbles.

Toddy and Al step back and watch the man in astonishment. He regains his breath and sits, panting, staring at the ground below him.

Al suddenly says, "His bag!" He leaps up on a rock and looks downstream. "I can see it," he says, then races off.

Al's quick departure takes Toddy by surprise, and he is

suddenly left alone with the naked man from the blue bubbles in the sky. He takes a step back, ready to make a run for it if he needs to.

The man places his hand on his face, grumbling in a strange language. Then he turns and observes Toddy standing there. Toddy backs up against a boulder and forces a nervous grin.

After what seems an age, Al returns with the bag, puffing. He sees the man sitting blinking in the sunlight. "Is he alright?"

"I think so."

Al takes a longing look at the shimmering bag and then offers it to the man. The man takes it from him, making a nod of the head in thanks.

Toddy moves closer and rests on his haunches, observing the man with fascination. "You freaked me out."

"Where'd you come from?" asks Al.

The man just smiles gently, exhibiting a confused frown. He looks around and sees the rocks, boulders, rainforest, and the clear, fast-flowing creek.

Slowly the man repeats what he has just heard, "Weredu-cunfrum." He mulls it over for a few seconds then asks, in Norwegian, "Snakker du Norsk?"

He receives only confused looks from Toddy and Al. So he tries another language.

"آپ کہاں سے آیا؟" the man asks in Urdu but he receives only more blank looks.

"What is your name?" asks Toddy.

The man smiles and says, "*Ahhh*. English."

"English. Your name is English?" asks Al.

"My name is English?" asks the man, confused.

"Is your name bloody English?" snaps Toddy, holding the man's shoulder and looking straight into his eyes.

The man looks at Toddy's hand on his shoulder "My name is not Bloody English," he says. "My name is Zemitheree Beden-ifictu."

"Heck," says Al. "That's one hell of a name."

For a moment there is a pause with the men looking at each other expectantly. All three burst into laughter.

"I am going to call you Zem," says Toddy.

"Okay," says Zem. He hugs ~~his~~ the bag against his belly and looks around at the creek.

"Where are we?"

"Alligator Creek," says Al.

"Alligator?" asks Zem thinking it through. "America?"

"No mate, Australia."

Zem looks confused. "There are crocodiles in Australia."

Toddy snaps, "Crocodiles in Australia but the creek's called Alligator. Hey, are you okay?"

Zen shudders, gasps. His body convulses, and he gags as though he is unable to breathe. His eyes widen and his face freezes. His body floods with adrenaline as he *becomes present*. His mind is overwhelmed by every noticeable sensation: the brilliant white clouds in the harsh blue sky, the warm breeze touching his skin, the white noise of the moving water, the two humans in such close proximity.

"Is this Earth?" Zem stammers, trying to catch his breath. He touches his hand to his forehead then looks at the bright red blood on his fingertips. Then he passes out on the pebble beach.

Earth Friends

Zem wakes in a bed in a darkened room. He sits up slowly, feeling the bump on his forehead under a rudimentary bandage. His body aches. He hears voices through the half-open door and recognizes that of Al and Toddy talking to another person, a female.

In the half-light, Zem sees his pouch at the foot of the bed sitting on top of a white cotton dressing gown. He stands, unsteadily, places his bag under the bed and picks up the gown. It is worse for wear, grubby and with a Hilton Hotels insignia. He dons the gown and opens the door and peers down the hallway to the source of the voices.

The house is old and untidy but homely. In the center of the lounge room there is a coffee table and a three-seat settee and two single armchairs. Toddy is at one end of the couch, rolling a cigarette; Al is slouched in an armchair.

Zem takes a few slow steps forward. He is a big presence in the hallway with a grubby white gown and a clean white bandage on his forehead.

"Hey dude," Al says excitedly. "Come in, man. Sit down."

Zem approaches and sees a young woman with an oval face and freckles on her nose sitting on the other end of the couch, her legs tucked under her body. She is smiling at him. She has wide brown eyes. Her hair is brown tinged with red or red tinged with brown, depending on the light. The redness clashes with her pale blue dress, which has a white collar and a name badge that reads: Megan.

Zem slowly lowers himself into the unoccupied armchair.

"Feeling better, brother?" Toddy asks.

"I feel like I fell through a wormhole," says Zem.

"This is what I reckon," says Al. "Old mate Zem, here, is military special operations, like Delta Fox or Navy Sealions. He's on a training mission in a stealth Black Hawk helicopter. They mess up the drop. Aand he ends up in the creek."

"Nice Yeah,!" says Toddy, enthusiastically. "Did you shoot Bin Laden, Zem?"

"Maybe," says Zem, not sure what they are talking about.

"Unfortunately, Al," Toddy continues. "There is a flaw in your hypothesis."

"What is that?" asks Megan.

"Any minute now, Zem's army buddies are going to bust through the door with their guns and we are all going to get shot for kidnapping him."

"I guess," agrees Al. "We need a better story."

"Do you have a better story, Zem?" asks Megan, reaching over to take the cigarette from Toddy.

"I like that one," says Zem.

"Really?" asks Toddy, "You want a rollie?"

"Yes, thank you," says Zem, not knowing what he is accepting.

"Here's my story," says Megan puffing smoke into the air. "Our friend Zem is a spaceman who has come down to help fix the irrigation system on the plantation so we can all get through the next semester without me having to work in cafés to pay the bills."

"That's a great story," says Al, enthusiastically. "Zem the cosmic cultivator from Planet Chop Chop."

"I'll buy that one," says Toddy. He hands Zem a thin cigarette saying, "there you go mate, home-grown. We bought these PV solar panels to run the irrigation pump. Can't figure out how to get them going. Know anything about solar panels, Zem?"

Zem is not concentrating; he is watching Megan draw from the cigarette. He tries the same technique with the one he has taken from Toddy and shortly, ~~in a second~~ he is coughing his guts out.

Al starts clapping, "Go virgin lungs!"

"Be nice," says Megan, rising from her seat. She places a hand on Zem's back, rubbing circles there. Zem stops coughing and his eyes meet her eyes.

"You okay now?"

Zem nods, noticing the smoothness and the perfume of her skin. Megan's aura tears a hole in the fabric of space-time and Zem *becomes present*. He feels the sensation of falling.

Toddy says, "So, Zemmy. Do you know anything about solar panels? Oh, shit! He's off again."

Zem is overwhelmed by a rush of hypersensitivity. Everything falls upon him at once: the dim room, the ashtray full of rollie butts in the centre of the wooden table; the heat of Megan's hand and the perfume of her breath; the humans chatting away. It's too much. His face is pale, and his eyes roll back. And there is a new sensation; something pounding on his back.

Toddy slaps him roughly, "Hey bro. Stay with us, okay."

"Toddy, be gentle!" shouts Megan, pushing Toddy away.

Zem sits back, exhausted. He clenches his fist around Megan's hand. "Is this Earth?" he asks breathlessly. "Is this what it's like?"

Al leans forward in his seat, elbows on his knees, his chin resting on his clasped hands. He is watching and listening intently. *What is this?*

"It's okay," says Megan. "You are okay here, Zem. Let me

take you back to bed."

Zem allows Megan to help him stand, and he sways for a few moments. Toddy resumes his seat and looks at Al who is watching Megan walk Zem down the hallway.

"You_all come back now," says Toddy comically, over his shoulder.

"We've got a live one, hey?" says Al.

"The things you find in the creek!

"Reckon we need a doctor?"

"If he's he doesn't die in his sleep, he should be fine."

In the spare room, Megan helps Zem into the bed. The darkness of the room and the silence is comforting.

"Toddy says that you fell out of the sky. Is that true?"

"I don't know," says Zem.

"Toddy is prone to making things up. But Al says that you fell out of the sky, too. So I don't know what to believe."

"I am glad that I am here," says Zem, softly.

Megan places her fingers on his forehead, checking that the bandage is holding in place. "Just sleep. Okay."

"Sleep?" he asks, like it was a foreign concept.

"Yeah, just sleep." Megan sits on the bed next to Zem. "Sleep is what you do when you close your eyes."

Megan sits with Zem for a while as he calms and his breathing returns to normal. Megan stands and pauses in the doorway smiling at him. She closes the door gently behind her.

Then through the closed door, Zem hears Megan say to Toddy and Al, "You guys are a blast." And then there is a peal of laughter.

Zem looks around in the gloom listening to the voices. So this is Earth, he thinks. *What am I doing here?*

When on Earth

The next day Zem wakes, still wearing the grubby cotton bathrobe. Megan is sitting on the side of the bed.

"Hi," she says, quietly.

"Hello Megan," Zem adjusts himself to sit upright.

"Well, aren't you Captain Snooze? Fourteen hours. Do you feel better?"

"I have pains."

Megan takes Zem's hand gently. "Show me where the pain is," she says and allows Zem to guide her hand first to his forehead, then to his shoulder where a bruise is showing, then to his belly.

"That last one is called hungry. How about I fix you some dippy eggs?"

"I don't know what that is."

"It's nice. Is this your bag?"

Megan shifts the pouch from under the bed with her foot so that Zem can see. "Very fancy pants. Can I see it?"

"Can you see it?"

"I mean can I take a look at it? Can I hold it?"

"Okay."

Megan retrieves the bag from the floor and places it on her lap ceremoniously. The material shimmers with rainbow colours and she runs her fingers across its surface. It feels like ~~snake skin~~snakeskin, slippery but not wet. She picks it up and turns it around trying to find the clasp or the opening through which things go in and out, but there is none.

"Wow," she says, genuinely surprised. "This is some man's bag. How do you get your man bits inside it?"

Zem looks on, nonplussed as Megan squeezes the bag like

11

the contents can be determined by touch. She shakes it next to her head, but there is no noise. Then she gives up, with a hint of frustration.

"It is a bag, isn't it?" she asks. "It's not a kidney from a dinosaur or something?"

Zem doesn't know how to reply so he says nothing.

"Anyway. Do you want coffee?" she places the bag on the bed next to her.

"Coffee," he asks. "I don't know. Maybe."

Megan smiles and says, "I'll make you coffee and some dippy eggs. See if you can break into your pouch."

Megan departs Zem's eyes fall on the bag, sitting at the foot of the bed. The bag is a mystery to him as well. He reaches for the bag observing the patterns on the material. He turns it to its correct orientation and the mouth of the bag falls open in his hands.

Zem shoots a cautious glance at the door. He puts his hand gingerly inside and feels objects of varying shapes and sizes. He gently fingers the contents, trying to piece it all together.

He leans from the bed and pushes the door closed, then arranges the bed sheets so that he can throw a cover over the bag at a second's notice. He empties the contents of the bag into a pile in front of him.

The sunlight wending its way through the window and reflecting off the walls in the room is sufficient to make the gold nuggets shine brilliantly. There are dozens of them.

Also glistening on the bed sheet are gemstones, each the size of a small bird's eggs. Zem examines one of the gems, peering at the clear crystal interlaced with fine strands of a silver-grey metal.

There are two glass vials, one containing a green powder

and the other a rust-coloured liquid. Also, a small ingot of lightweight, industrial-looking metal. And there is a transparent box containing a thin crystalline material, like wafers of silica.

The final item is a device that looks like a remote control on crystal meth. Zem turns it around in his hands baffled as to its purpose.

He replaces the objects in the bag, all but three of the gold nuggets that he places in the pocket of his grubby Hilton Hotels bathrobe. As if in tune with his thoughts, the bag closes once the last item is inside.

Zem stands, pushing the bag under the bed with his foot. He steps into the ~~hall-way~~hallway just as Megan approaches, heading out the back door with a pair of scissors.

"Bathroom is there," she says, nodding in the direction of an open door.

Unlike the rest of the house, the bathroom is relatively clean. Zem observes the vanity basin, seeing water dripping from the tap. He bathes his face. He stands, wiping water away and sees his reflection in the mirror.

Who is that person? This place? The white tiles; and the bright light outside flooding through the windows. The hard cold floor; the yellow rusty colour where the water touches the side of the hand basin.

Zem's mind falls into the deep end, unable to swim. He is *getting present* again, but he holds himself. There is a clattering noise of the fly-screen as Megan returns with herbs from the garden.

Get a grip, Zemitheree, this is just the beginning. But then he is confused. *The beginning of what?* He inhales deeply then exhales slowly. Oxygen floods his cells and his composure returns.

He pulls the bandage away from his head and examines the wound. It is not deep, and it is no longer bleeding. He studies the reflection in the mirror. Is that Zemitheree Beden-ifictu? He looks terrible. And what the hell is he wearing? Is this Earth clothing?

Zem steps back into the hallway adjusting the grubby Hilton Hotel bathrobe. Al and Toddy are seated at the kitchen bench waiting for Megan to serve up lunch.

"Hey, Zem, buddy," says Al, enthusiastically. "How did you sleep?"

"Sleep?" asks Zem, pondering the word. "I feel like something trod on me. But the sun is shining, and my Earth friends are still alive. It is good to be here."

"You sure talk a lot when you wake up," says Toddy. He slaps Zem on the arm. "Sit down Bro. Megan's done dippy eggs."

"As always," says Megan.

"You ever had dippy eggs before?" asks Al, shoving a piece of wet toast into his mouth.

"I don't think so," says Zem, watching the precise manner in which Megan scoops the egg white and yolk from the shell with a thin slice of toast. Zem finds this very strange.

And as if that wasn't odd enough, all three of Zem's companions are inserting the toast with dippy egg into their mouths crushing it with their teeth and then swallowing it. *Swallowing it!*

Zem observes that Toddy has a piece of toast gripped between his teeth. When their eyes meet, Toddy removes the toast and places it on the bench as though he were going to make a statement. Impatiently, Toddy clears his throat, as though he were speaking for Al and Megan too.

"Where exactly are you from, Zemmy?"

If only he knew an honest answer. Zem observes Al and Megan watching him. He is on the spot now.

Zem clears his throat, "Where was I between being on that couch with the home-grown and being in the bed a little while ago?" he asks honestly, looking at his three friends in turn.

Toddy pulls a face as though it were a weird question, "Zem. You were just in the bed, asleep."

"Did I leave at any stage?"

"I don't think so. Did he?" asks Al.

Megan places her fingers on Zem's hand, leaning forward, "Did you go somewhere?" she asks, concerned. Zem observes the fine hairs on her forearms have become erect and the skin is speckled with tiny lumps. The room suddenly seems silent.

Zem says, slowly, thinking hard to recall details, "I was in a room. It was vast and very clean. I was standing against a white block. I had to take off this gown. I was naked. And in front of me was a woman, she was old but noble, and had the most exquisite prosthetic adornments."

"Prosthetic what?" asks Al.

"*Shhh*," Megan hisses.

Zem continues, "She was senior. There was an argument. Then this man gave her the bag, the one under the bed. And then this bright blue light. And then..." Zem sits back, his eyes wide open as though the lids were glued open. He gasps.

Megan, Toddy, and Al have their breaths held, mesmerized. Not daring to speak. Their eyes flit back and forth, their minds locked in a deep mystery. Megan's lips tremble as if she were trying to speak.

Toddy grunts and slaps his hand on the counter. "He was dreaming! Look at you guys. *Doodee-doodle. Doodee-doodle.* It's not the Twilight Zone. Zem had a dream."

Megan exhales, exhausted. "You nearly killed me, Zem. I was waiting for the woman with the thingy to come in here and get us."

"That was awesome," says Al. "Look at my goosebumps. "Man, it's so cool having Zem in the house. We should clone him and lease them out. We'd make a fortune."

"I don't understand," says Zem.

"You were dreaming, mate," Toddy barks. "You fell asleep and you had a dream. You go places in your head. Don't they have dreams where you come from?"

Al says, "Zem's not a spaceman. He's just some Schwarzenegger dude who's lost his memory."

"Of course," says Megan. "You get a lot of amnesiacs falling out of blue bubbles into Alligator Creek this time of year."

"Well who is he then?" continues Toddy. "He's built like a machine. Mate, if he goes ~~bad~~bad, he'll tear us apart."

"He's right here!" protests Megan.

Zem is following the argument as best he can. He doesn't want to fall out of favour with his Earth friends, so he follows their custom. He spears the soldier's leg into the egg and shoves it into his mouth.

Toddy is winding up, "I'm okay having a spaceman in the house but he has to figure out who he is pretty quickly!"

Zem gives the dippy egg three good chews like Megan did and then swallows. Down his throat, it goes. *And straight back up again!*

Zem spews up across the kitchen counter and a big blob of

toast-egg-vomit hits Toddy in the chest.

"Bugger! There's a puking spaceman in the kitchen!" Toddy shrieks, stumbling off his stool.

"He's not a spaceman!" shouts Megan, moving to help Zem clean up with a dis cloth.

"Sorry about that," says Zem, wiping yolk off his chin.

"No worries, bro," snaps Toddy, snidely "Nothing like a bit of alien spew in your lunch. Who the f**k are you, Zem?"

"I don't know," says Zem, defensively.

"Toddy, leave him," says Megan.

"No. Where are you from, Zem?" Toddy pushes his finger into Zem's chest.

Zem is taken aback by Toddy's aggression, and he bellows, "I DON'T KNOW WHO I AM!"

Toddy almost falls over. He raises his hands defensively, "Who! All right, bro."

"I don't know who I am!" repeats Zem. "But I am here for a reason. Something important. And I don't know what it is."

"Leave him, Toddy," says Megan, quietly.

Toddy slowly takes his seat again and rocks back looking at the counter. He thinks for a few seconds then, without meeting his Zem's eyes he places his hand on Zem's wrist. Not gently, the way Megan does, but with a hard pat and squeeze, like a fighter's truce. "You're okay mate," says Toddy. "Just watch where you spew next time."

Toddy gets off his seat, and moves away from the bench muttering, "I'm going to fix the solar panels."

Al and Megan watch him go while Zem gently brushes toast crumbs off his lap.

"He's such a hot-head," says Al, as Toddy lets the fly-screen clang shut behind him.

"His head gets steamy," Megan says. "Nothing but gas in there. Are you okay, Zem?"

"Yeah. I'm okay. Sorry about the... You know."

Megan takes both his hands hers and looks into his eyes, "You are welcome here, okay, by all of us. You don't have to tell us anything, but if you remember anything, we are dying to know."

"Me too," says Zem.

"Now you want to have another go with the dippy egg? It will help with the pain in your stomach."

With some coaching, Zem is able to get an entire egg and slice of toast to stay down. The second egg is easier. He is on his third egg when Toddy walks into the lounge room and tosses a bundle of papers on the table and sits down on the sofa.

"I am going to roll up. Want a smoke spaceman?" he says.

Zem is feeling pretty good with the eggs and toast inside him. He doesn't know what roll-up means, but nonetheless says, "Yeah. Sure." He takes a seat next to Toddy. He picks up the document from the coffee table. "Is this your solar project?"

"Yeah. Four solar panels, a pump, a battery and some wires. The pump either goes mad like it's going to burn out, or it just dribbles. Useless, expensive rubbish."

Zem examines the document and Toddy looks at him, hopefully. "Give it a nudge if you want. It's out the back."

"I might have a look." Zem takes the documents and walks outside in his Hilton Hotels bathrobe.

When he returns, Megan and Al are in their normal seats. Zem approaches and Megan sees he is drenched. She falls apart laughing.

Toddy looks round. He won't laugh out loud, but can't stop from smiling like a Cheshire Cat. "Don't tell me," he says.

"The little black tubes are spraying water now."

Al stops laughing long enough to say, "I tell you. He's a cosmic electrician."

"You are a totally awesome dude. Sit down. Here, have a drag on this," Toddy takes the cigarette from Al and passes it to Zem. "Don't get it wet."

"How did you do it?" asks Megan.

"I just _did what seemed to make sense_ ~~connected them one plus one divided by two plus two~~," says Zem~~, not knowing if that makes any sense.~~

~~"Series and parallel," says Al. "Of course."~~

"Whatever," says Toddy. "It works!"

"Can you fix hairdryers as well?" ~~asks~~ Megan _asks, smugly_.

"Maybe," says Zem, bashfully. "Hey, listen I want to say something." He puts his hand inside the pocket of his wet Hilton Hotels bathrobe. "I have a problem. I don't know who I am or how I came to be here, but I have a strong conviction that everything is okay and it's all for a reason. And if I continue to seek, I will find the answer."

Zem looks at his three friends in turn. He retrieves his hand from his pocket and lays the three gold nuggets that he found in his bag on the table, next to the ashtray full of rollie butts. "I don't know what value they have."

"Are they gold," asks Megan picking up one of the nuggets, inspecting its sheen in the light.

"I think so."

"Were these in your bag?" asks Toddy.

"Yes."

"Good thing we fished it out of the creek, hey?" says Al.

Zem shows a blank look and Al says, "When you fell in the creek you lost your bag. I had to go running for it. I nearly lost it in the rapids."

Zem frowns upon hearing this. He grits his teeth. He cannot risk losing the bag again.

"Are these for us?" asks Megan, hopefully.

"Yes. Would you consider it a payment for being my friends?" says Zem, and he is surprised to see Megan drop the nugget back on the table.

"Sorry, Zem, you don't get to buy my friendship," she snaps.

The tone of her voice is strange to Zem, and he looks ~~perplexed~~furrows his brow. Megan sits back with her arms folded across her chest and an accusing frown.

"Food and accommodation," says Al.

"Yeah," says Toddy. "It's like rent. Not like old mate needs to pay rent now he's fixed the irrigation."

"Rent?" asks Zem of Megan. Her frown gives way to a cheeky smile, and she leans forward and retrieves her nugget, holding it against her cheek.

"Okay Zem. I'll be your friend because I like you. And I'll be your landlady because you have crossed my palm with gold."

"What do you reckon these are worth?" asks Al.

"You can't sell it. It's a gift," says Megan.

"You have one of your own, don't you Zem?" asks Toddy.

"Yes. And please. Sell them if you wish," says Zem. Then a thought comes to him. "What might they be worth?"

"Dunno. What are they? ~~I A~~ fifty grams?" says Toddy.

"Mine's fifty-one," says Megan, holding the nugget against

the top of her breast as though it were a pendant. She looks at Zem in a manner he had not seen before. Her pupils seem wider than normal and Zem feels an odd sensation under his bathrobe. Zem sees moisture glistening on her lips.

"What's gold selling for now?" asks Toddy.

"Send a text to old mate Danio," says Megan to Al. "He runs that pawn shop. He'll know. And Toddy. Get the scales, we'll weight them."

Toddy and Al do as instructed.

"You okay, Zem?" asks Megan.

Zem realizes that he has been staring at her mouth. He looks away, embarrassed.

"Looks like you parked up there for a minute," she says, smiling seductively.

Zem comes out of his trance and shakes his head. "What's happening?" he asks.

Megan says, "I have the houseboys running errands. You just need to feed them. Then you can ~~Feed them and you can~~ tell them what to do."

That's good advice. Zem rests back in the sofa, adjusting the lapel of his wet Hilton Hotels.

Toddy returns with the scales. He settles ~~and weighs the first~~ a gold nugget on the metal tray and squints at the electronic readout. "Okay, first one is 33.3 grams."

"Write that down, Al," says Megan, and he complies.

"Number two is 33.3 grams."

"That must be some sort of cosmic coincidence," says Al, taking the two weighed nuggets and examining them closely.

"Okay, Megan, number three."

"Isn't for sale."

"Let's weight it anyway."

"Alright but don't mix them up. Mine is unique."

"They can't be unique if they weigh the same. Hand it over."

"Actually, they are unique," says Al. "They are both nuggety, but nonetheless, distinct. Look."

"Megan's nugget is… 33.3 grams. I don't believe it."

"I win," says Megan, excitedly. "Give it back, Toddy. Thank you Zem. This is a beautiful gift."

Al's text goes off and he reads the message, "Here we go. Old mate from the pawnshop says he'll give us 90 dollars a gram."

Megan says. "Nice. Then that's about $3,000 each for you two, because mine is not for sale."

"Three grand! Wow! Thanks, Zem," says Al.

Toddy turns to Zem and says formally, "Thanks for this, Zemmy. It's a great gesture. I apologize for blowing up at lunch." He offers his hand.

"Me too," says Al leaning across the table to shake.

"Me too, as well," says Megan and she leans over and gives Zem a kiss on the cheek instead of a handshake. Zem feels a sense of paralysis as she approaches and has her way with him. It is both scary and nice at the same time.

Toddy takes the un-smoked cigarette from Zem's fingers, lights it, takes a long drag from it and, passes it back to Zem, exhaling blue smoke.

"Oh, man," Toddy says, clapping his hands together. "This is so awesome. We've got a spaceman in the house. The irrigation is fixed; a bumper crop of Chop-Chop on the way. Gold nuggets. Three grand. What's next?"

"Check him out," says Megan indicating towards Zem.

Zem is the center of attention again; his eyebrows curl up

in a question mark. Sitting there in his damp and grubby Hilton Hotels dressing gown, grinning. The dippy egg digesting in his stomach, the first thing he had eaten in his entire life. Zem is most definitely on Earth.

"A penny for your thoughts," says Megan.

"Huh? "says Zem

"What are you thinking?"

"I am thinking that I like this planet. What are you thinking?"

"I'm thinking you need some proper clothes," says Al.

Pawn Shop

Next day, Megan and Zem are in an old Ford Falcon
utility, driving north towards Townsville. It is a bright sunny
day and Zem wears borrowed clothes, looking less like Hugh
Heffner and more like Huckleberry Finn, cut down jeans and
a t-shirt with a rude cartoon on the front.

As they approach the City, Zem peers out the window,
taking an interest in the buildings in the distance.

"Okay, so this is the plan," says Megan. "We go to the
pawnshop, cash in the three nuggets, yours, Al's, and
Toddy's, buy you some clothes, go to the university library,
get the books we need, then we go back home. How's that?"

"It's good. What's that?" asks Zem pointing out the
window at tall buildings.

"That's the C.B.D. The central business district."

"Are they the biggest buildings in this town?"

"The tallest. The shopping center we are going to is really
big. But only one storey."

"What do they do there?" asks Zem, as the ute approaches
the City Center.

"It's where it all happens," she says.

"Like the administrative center?"

"Something like that. Does it remind you of something?"

"I don't know."

"Anyway, let's take a detour." Megan turns right on
Flinders East, and drives towards the Strand. There is a
marina with ornate apartment buildings overlooking the
boats.

"What happens here?" asks Zem intrigued by the buildings.

"Condos. People live there. Gorgeous aren't they"

"I like it," he says.

"Bit out of our price range."

"How does it work between you and Toddy," asks Zem.

Megan blushes, "We just hang out together. Share some classes at Uni." Megan thinks for a while then says honestly, "Toddy and I shack up occasionally."

Zem looks at her and she makes an embarrassed smile. She says, "Nothing serious. Toddy's not really serious about anything."

"Are you serious about anything?" asks Zem.

"Not really. You?" she replies defensively.

"Yes, very. I just don't know what. Can we go inside?"

"The apartment buildings? I doubt they will let us in."

"Why wouldn't they?"

"Dressed like this?" Megan indicates her threadbare frock and Zem's tee shirt. "What's the time? Okay. We could come back on the way home. I'll ring them, make an appointment."

Megan drives along the Strand, the parkland along the waterfront. Zem looks at the people walking, the buildings and the vehicles. He observes a woman with a small dog doing its business on the grass. The owner picks up the poo with a bag over his hand. Zem looks at Megan with a confused frown and she just shrugs.

Megan turns off the Strand and Zem continues to observe with interest the coming and goings of the town. Eventually, Megan parks the car on the street outside the pawn shop.

"This is the place," she says as she pulls the handbrake on tight.

They enter the shop together. It is dimly lit, full of stuff: instruments, utensils, tools, and jewelry jewellery. There is a glass counter covered in documents and an overflowing

25

ashtray. Adding to the ashtray is an old, gaunt man with sagging skin, thick glasses, and nicotine stains on the inside of the fingers of his right hand. The man looks Megan and Zem up and down, as though he were trying to figure out what she would be doing with him, and why he would be dressed that way.

"We spoke to Danio the other day. Is he here?" asks Megan.

"No," says the gaunt man, gruffly.

"Danio says that you pay ninety dollars a gram for gold."

"Eighty," says the gaunt man.

"Danio says ninety," says Megan.

"I ain't f**king Danio, lady," says the man, curtly. "Are you?"

Zem looks at the old man, surprised at his tone of voice. He looks at Megan, confused. She indicates that he should bring out the nuggets. Zem places a single nugget on the glass counter. The pawnbroker picks it up and examines it with an eyeglass. He twirls it this way and that, then places it on a set of scales, "33 grams."

Zem shoulders pull back and he snarls, "33.3 grams."

"I don't buy decimals."

Zem takes a moment to observe the man. He can smell ~~the~~ his breath and sees specks of food caught between his teeth. Zem wants to euthanize him right there. Instead, he moves towards the shop window and retrieves a sign he had seen on the way in. He raises the sign in the air and slams it on the glass counter with such force that the documents and the ashtray fly into the air in a cloud of ash.

The scrawny man gasps as Zem leans across the counter, grips him by the collar and draws him so close that the tips of their noses touch. "I have three friends on Earth. Don't become my first enemy"

The scrawny man looks out of the corner of his eye to see the sign that reads: *We buy Gold $90/gram.*

Zem pushes him away, retrieves two more nuggets from his pocket and places these next to the first on the scales. He stands back, places his hand in his pocket, looks at the floor and says, "Megan."

Megan steps breathlessly forward, retrieves a piece of paper from her pocket and recites the numbers that Al had written on it, "3 nuggets at 33.3 grams each, at $90 per gram is $8,991.

The gaunt man is trembling, his eyes shifting left and right. He says, "I didn't know you had so much."

Zem extends his hand to the pawnshop attendant. The man reluctantly shakes, and Zem holds his hand firmly, creating the sensation that the hand may never be returned. "Let's round it up to $9000."

"I need a key," says the gaunt man. He is trembling as he retrieves a ring of keys from a drawer and then shuffles into another room. He returns with a pile of cash and counts it out on the glass top. "There's $9,000," he says almost glad to give the money away.

"Nice doing business with you," Zem takes up the cash, and hands it to Megan. He places his hand in the small of Megan's back and directs her out of the pawnshop.

In the car Megan recounts the money and announces, "$9,000 thousand dollars. It's all there."

"That was fun, *huh*?"

"Fun? I thought that you were going to kill him."

"I wouldn't have killed him unless he threatened to harm

us," Zem says matter-of-factly. "In that case I would have pushed his head through the counter and cut his throat open on the broken glass."

Megan freezes, remembering a comment that Zem made in the house the day before. Something about his Earth friends still being alive.

Zem notices her demeanour. "Are you okay?"

"Please tell me you didn't just say that."

Megan's eyes show the same expression as when he offered to buy her friendship with the gold nugget. Al helped him out of the situation. Al isn't here now.

"What's that expression you use? The one with the goat?"

"Just kidding."

"I was just kidding."

Megan tucks the wad of cash into the glove box, and fires the engine of the ute. She drives to the shopping center in silence.

Clothes Shopping

Megan parks the car on the rooftop of the shopping center and walks with Zem to the escalator. As they are descending into the building, Megan announces, "I think I need a coffee."

Seated at a table in the cafe shop, Megan is distracted. A waitress delivers two flat white coffees. Zem sniffs the drink unsure whether or not to drink it. He observes Megan's demeanour, concerned that the flow between the has stopped.

"The agenda," he says. "We sold the gold. Now we buy some clothes, right?"

"Have you ever bought clothes before?" she Megan asks nervously, and then realizes that it is a silly question. "Never mind. Do you know what you would like to wear?"

"What I have been wearing until now has seemed very informal," Zem says, resting back in his chair, revealing the image on his tee-shirt, a cartoon of a dog holding up its middle claw with the caption, "Swivel, Bitch."

Suddenly, being with Zem isn't scary anymore. "You mean the bathrobe?" she starts laughing, remembering him walking into the lounge room, drenched. She picks up her cup akwardly awkwardly, and spills coffee on the table. "Do you have any idea what it is like being around you?" She mops up spilt coffee with a napkin. "You are turning my world upside down."

"How is that working for you?"

"Fun. Scary. Terrifying. Amazing."

"That's good, huh?"

"You're the spaceman with a bag full of gold. You are the

architect. Is it good? Does it end well?"

Zem leans forward, his right arm resting on the table, his face close to Megan's, "You know what?"

"What?"

"I have just had an incredible insight."

"Which is?"

"I come from a race of very dull, serious people. You humans are awesome. Every day's an adventure."

"Let me tell you something, buddy," says Megan. "There's nothing dull about you."

After the coffee, Megan leads Zem into the shopping center and pulls him to a halt outside a surf-wear shop. He looks at the clothes in the window display without really connecting.

Megan says, "Maybe we go like this. Just walk around and if you see anything you would like to wear, just buy it. You have plenty of money, there's no haggling here."

"Do you want some money?" Zem asks, retrieving a bundle of cash from his pocket, his share of the $9,000.

"I'm fine. I have my commission"

"Commission?

"Ten percent from Toddy and Al for selling the nuggets and getting their books from the library. That's the good thing about lazy men; they will pay anything to do nothing. Actually, I should probably give you half of my cut."

"Call it rent."

"More rent? Really?"

"So, if I see something I like I just go into the shop and ask them to sell it to me?"

"Maybe it's best if I come with you."

"Okay. Let's do that."

"Alright then." Megan looks in the window display of the surf shop they are standing next to. "What about this?" she asks, indicating a pair of board shorts.

"*Hmmm*," says Zem.

"What about that t-shirt. The one with the shark on it."

"*Ummm.*"

"Oh, wow. Check out the hoodie."

Zem takes Megan's hand and says, "Megan. If our agreement is that when 'I' see something that 'I' like, 'I' should buy it, why are you trying to impress upon me the things that you like?"

Megan looks nonplussed. She scratches her eyebrow with a fingernail and says quietly, "I don't think this is going to work."

"It will work fine," says Zem.

Zem takes Megan's hand in his. She looks at it mistrustfully for a moment then lets him tow her through the shopping center at a brisk pace. Megan is exhausted by the time they have completed the circuit and come to a stop in front of the shop where Zem wants to buy.

"This is the place," Zem says confidently, looking at the dressed manikins in the window.

"I'm not sure how this will go to down at home," says Megan.

"There is a dress code in your house?"

"More of a fashion code, really."

"Well, this is me," says Zem, confidently. "Coming?"

"I'll meet you in the coffee shop when you're finished."

Zem's shopping spree is the highlight of the week for the shop attendant. Thirty minutes of intense activity: measuring, checking racks, trying on, choosing, and eventually transacting over two thousand dollars.

Zem walks back to the coffee shop carrying shopping bags, where he sees Megan wearing a new version of what she was wearing before. He stands in front of her in his new outfit, but she looks right through him.

"Megan. You look awesome."

"*Uhhh!* Zem."

"Did you get a new dress?"

"No, I…. What are you wearing?"

"Navy pinstripe."

"Why are you wearing a suit?"

"You know that's a very good question." Zem places his bags on the ground a takes a seat across the table from Megan. He is contemplative for a long pause then asks rhetorically, "Why did I buy this suit? What is driving my actions? Why did I give away the gold nuggets and not slaughter you all on the first night?"

"Are you f**king serious?" Megan stands instantly, but she is unable to move away from the table.

"I am sorry, Megan. I'm sorry."

"I can't believe that you just said that."

Zem is anxious. He needs her complicity. Something crucial needs to be conveyed. He reaches out for Megan's hand, feeling pulse racing through her skin. "Please sit down, Megan," he says calmly. "Please."

Slowly, Megan returns to her chair.

"Megan. I don't know who I am. Yet, I have convictions that are as tangible as the material objects that surround us. In the same way that this table is here, I know that it was right that I bought this suit, and that I gave you the gold."

"And that you didn't murder us on the first night," Megan

says. "Or cut the old man's throat in the pawn shop?"

Zem sits back. Where is she going with this?

Moisture glistens in the corner of Megan's eyes. She taps her fingernail repeatedly on the table and speaks with a faltering voice. "I am glad you had no conviction to murder us on the first night. But what happens to me or Al or Toddy when you figure out your agenda. Do you kill us then?"

The Mouse

No words are spoken on the drive from the shopping center to the university library. Megan pulls the car to a halt in the car park and sits looking at her hands quietly. "Zem, will you promise me something?"

"Okay."

"Will you stop talking about killing your friends? Even if it is in the context of. *I would never kill my friends.* You being so odd is kinda funokay. But potential murderer is really uncomfortable."

"I understand."

"And maybe you could stop talking about killing enemies, too. Even if your mission were to kill oilmen and billionaires, I'd still prefer you didn't talk about it. Okay?"

"Okay."

"Thank you," Megan meets Zem's eyes and her relieved smile suggests that the tension has passed.

Megan steps out of the car and Zem feels a wave of relief wash over him. Minutes later he is seated in a comfy chair in the library lobby thinking about Megan's emotional turn. Why was she so upset about him talking about killing? Who are these people anyway? And what would he do if it turned out that his objective and their wellbeing were mutually exclusive, as Megan had suggested? Would he kill them all? He chews the questions over and concludes that there is no answer, particularly as he so needs their help now. So he resolves to protect everything that he knows has value including Megan, Al, Toddy, the irrigation system, the chop-chop plants, and his bag. And if it turns out that his mission requires these things to be destroyed, he will deal with that later.

Megan appears before him with a pile of books cradled in her arms. Instantly, Zem's objectivity vanishes, and his only inclination is to be present to the exhilarating sensation of her company.

She is in high spirits, having had some time for her own soul searching. "I've got half the books. I have to get the other half. Is that alright?"

"It's good," says Zem, smiling.

"Are you okay sitting there? Do you want to go online?"

"Online?"

"The internet. I can log you onto a terminal."

"I don't know what that is."

"Come on. I think you'll like it."

Megan leads Zem to a row of computers and logs in. She says, "Sit down. I'll show you how it works. Okay, so this is called a browser. Grab the mouse."

"The mouse. Are you serious?"

"It's not a real mouse," she laughs. "Move it like this. See the cursor. Okay. Click here. Click, with your finger on the mouse."

"This is really funny," Zem, lets Megan's hand guide his.

"It would be funny if you were from outer space. But it's pretty routine for a uni-student. Anyway, whatever you want, write the word in here. Then press 'Enter'. Whenever the arrow turns into a hand, you can click the mouse and go to more information. Got it?"

"I think so."

"Good. I have to get Al's books now."

Zem watches Megan disappear amid the rows of shelves. He looks around at the architecture in the big old library and wonders what does he most want to know about? Humans.

He types the letters h-u-m-a-n-s on the keyboard and hits enter. Instantly on the computer monitor there are rows of text about humans. Zem moves the mouse, and this causes the cursor to move and to become a hand. He clicks the mouse and there appears a fifty-page document all about humans. Zem figures out how to scroll down the page. At page fifteen he is running through the aisles, looking for Megan, excitedly.

He finds her searching through a row of sociology textbooks. Zem is excitable and she thinks he might burst.

"Whoa, Zem, whoa," she says. "What's the matter?"

"How do I turn it into a book?"

"What?"

"The internet information. How do I turn it into a book?"

"You mean print it?"

"I don't know."

"You want that information on pieces of paper?"

"Yes, yes."

Megan retrieves her library card and holds it up in front of his face and says, "Listen to these instructions very carefully."

Zem takes the card and holds it reverentially and listens hard.

Megan says, "Swipe the card in the slot in the black box next to the computer. Then, simultaneously press the button that says C.T.R.L. and the button that says P. Okay. A big thing happens on the screen. Then press enter. Got it?"

Zem has it. He makes his way back to the computer terminals.

An hour passes before Megan returns with an armful of books. She stands, amazed at what she sees.

Zem has commandeered five terminals and is paying cash for students to locate and print documents for him. Reams of paper pour out of the printers and one of Zem's new employees dutifully collects and binds these documents.

There is something seriously wrong with this situation, Megan thinks. She retrieves her library card from Zem and checks out her pile of books. Then she retrieves Zem and checks him out of the library.

Back in the car, Zem excitedly flicks through his pile of documents, purring like a cat.

"What have you got?" asks Megan, glancing at the documents that have been bound with clear plastic covers.

"The internet is amazing," says Zem. "Everything is there."

"Read the titles to me," says Megan, "One by one." She looks over at Zem and is struck by the continual layering of his character in such a short space of time. First, supposedly appearing out of thin air, next washed up in the creek, naked. ~~Next~~Then, dishevelled in a wet dressing gown having fixed the irrigation. Then handing out gold ~~nuggets~~and relieving all the financial stress. Then dressed in a corporate suit. Now cradling documents like an academic. And all the time, a potential mass murderer in waiting. What's next? Megan wonders.

Zem sorts through the pile on his lap and reads the title of the top document, "First one is titled *Humanity: progress to date.*"

"A short story," ~~says~~ Megan quips.

"~~The~~ *United Nations Human Development Report.*"

"Work in progress. Next one."

"*The Millennium Ecosystem Assessment. The Global Petroleum Industry. International Finance.* And this one," says Zem, holding up a document, instantly engrossed in its contents.

Megan glances across as he thumbs through the pages, tight-knit text, lots of formulas and tables. "What's that one?"

"*Physics and Economics of High Temperature Superconductors.*"

"Is that it?" Megan is confused as to the connective tissue between them all.

"One more. *Algae biofuels. Potential and challenges.*"

Zem tidies the pile of documents and places them at his feet. He looks out the window of the car, smiling.

"Why couldn't you just download the last issue of Men's Health or an e-book," Megan asks, airily.

"Conviction, Megan. I went where it seemed right to go. That is an amazing thing that internet. You think we can get an internet?"

Megan pulls the car to a halt outside the apartment block overlooking the marina. "Just in time."

"For what?"

"Property inspection."

Outside the property manager's office, Megan pulls Zem to a halt and says, "I think you should lead. You do the talking."

"Why?"

"You remember this morning. I told you about their dress code. Well, after our shopping trip, I still look like me and you look like a banker."

"What are we here for?"

"You said you wanted to look at the apartments."

"Yes. Okay. Great. Are you ready?"

"I'm ready. Just walk in and lay on the charm."

Zem pushes open the door of the Property Manager's office. A middle-aged woman stands from behind a desk, holding out her hand. "You must be the three o'clock."

"Yes, we are," says Zem.

"Great. Well what can we do for you?"

Zem pulls back his shoulders and, with a high tone, says, "We want to inspect your most prestigious apartment. It must have an exceptional view, affording its inhabitants both sunrise and the sunset. An apartment protected from the elements and yet accessible to the cool breeze and the warmth of the sun."

The Property Agent frowns at Megan and she blushes.

"Uncle Zem is from Melbourne," she says, hopefully.

"A lot of people ask about the Penthouse. Tire-kickers mostly," says the Property Agent, defensively.

Megan retrieves a thick wad of cash from her handbag and lets the property agent see it. "Assuming that the apartment meets Uncle Zem's approval, we can only pay six months in advance. Is that okay?"

The property agent looks at the bundle of cash, then at Megan, then at Uncle Zem. Instantly she becomes active, fossicking around in a drawer. She locates the penthouse key and a brochure describing the apartment.

Zem and Megan walk out of the Agent's office and stand in front of the steel doors of an elevator.

"It's a fantastic elevator," says Zem.

"You can stop pitching now," Megan chuckles.

The Penthouse is immaculate and expansive. Zem walks through each of the rooms then unlocks the sliding doors to the balcony and steps outside.

After Megan has finished her investigations, she joins him on the balcony. "It's definitely a step up from the shack at Alligator Creek," she says.

"How much money is it to live here?" asks Zem.

"In your currency, it is about a gold nugget a week."

"What should we offer?"

"Two-thirds of a nugget.

"Would you like to live here?"

"Sure. But for you, that is probably a simple calculation. But for me, not so much."

"Why not?"

"Well for a start, I don't make enough money to live here, and assuming that you were to offer to pay for it, I would be indebted to you and I don't know if I want that. Also, I live with my friends Al and Toddy, and I like that. They are easily managed and there is a lot of reciprocity and I know their motivations, basic as they are. A move like would change that."

"Is that it?" asks Zem.

"No. Secondly. We live in a shack, and it doesn't matter if we spill things or break things because it's just a shack. This place wouldn't work unless it was kept immaculate. I could adjust to immaculate, Al could too, but Toddy would kick a fit."

"Anything else?" asks Zem.

"Well, it is a lot closer to uni, which is a bonus. Al would love it. And there are four rooms. And it's air-conditioned."

"Well that's a good thing," says Zem.

Megan wanders back inside the apartment for a while. When she returns, Zem is leaning against the balcony observing the across the water to Magnetic Island.

She moves next to him, excited and nervous. "Zem. You want to live here with us. And you can provide the money. Is that your conviction?"

"Absolutely."

"And what would you expect of us in return?"

"If I knew that my three Earth friends were close by, I would need nothing else. It would help me find my way."

"This would change things between me and Toddy."

"Is that a problem?"

"Well, you know. Can you afford all the nuggets?"

"Yes."

"If we lived here, we would need to maintain the place."

"I'll pay someone for that. You won't need to work to live."

"Okay. I'll talk to Al and Toddy."

The Thief

It is early evening when Megan pulls the ute to a stop outside the shack. In the normal parking place is another car, a Holden Torana with metallic paint and an air scoop on the bonnet.

"Who is that?" asks Zem.

"That's Danio's car. The guy who wasn't at the Pawn Shop." Megan leaves the motor running, looking at Danio's car, her finger taps repeatedly on the steering wheel.

"Is something the matter?"

"The bust-up in the Pawn Shop. Give me a few minutes to there's no bushfires burning."

Zem looks around at the trees. "There is no fire here."

"A metaphorical bushfire."

Zem remains in the car listening to the clicking noise as the motor cools. He returns and opens his door.

"Danio's got a stick up his ass."

"A metaphorical stick?"

"Unfortunately, yes. Don't kill him, okay?"

"Okay."

"And maybe leave all the bags and documents in the car for now. It's complicated enough as it is."

Megan returns to the house, announcing, "Guess who won the fashion contest."

Zem enters the lounge navy pinstripe and crocodile leather shoes.

"Wow, Zem! Check you out," says Al, excitedly.

Toddy has a unlit rollie hanging out of his mouth. He claps his hands together, "Love it. Love it. The Hilton bathrobe made an impression on you."

"Hey Zem, this is Danio," Al says.

Danio is seated next to Toddy on the couch. He is heavyset, mid-thirties, wearing an AC/DC t-shirt and jeans. He looks at Zem's extended hand, scowling.

"Mister nugget," says Danio, curtly.

"Who was that old guy in the Pawn Shop?" asked Megan.

"That was my uncle. Not a happy chicken. Who is this guy, anyway?"

Toddy leans forward, keen to dial down the tension, "He's old mate and he's hanging with us. Hey, Zem. Park up, buddy." Toddy indicates for Zem to sit in Megan's chair at the end of the couch.

From the kitchen Megan is watching events with a quite frown. "Anyone want a beer?" she asks. She retrieves a six-pack of stubbies and pulls the bottles out of the carboard wrapper "You want a beer, Danio?"

"No. I want to know what happened in the shop today."

Megan hands a beer to Toddy and Al. She opens a stubby and hands it to Zem.

"Actually, let me tell you what happened," says Danio. "You've lost your balls, Toddy. Old mate here has got your girl. He's buying you out. He's beating up on your mates. What are these things, anyway?" Danio takes the three gold nuggets out of his trouser pocket and tosses them onto the coffee table. "Never seen anything like them."

Zem leans forward, now acutely interested in events. What's happening, here. Why is Danio upset? Why is he projecting aggression? Who is this guy anyway? Friend or foe?

Toddy lights his rollie, takes a drag, and then stubs it out in the ashtray. "Is there something you want to tell us, Danio?"

Danio retrieves the gold nuggets. "All good, Toddy. I should get going. Need a piss first."

"Piss away, dude. Down the hall."

Zem listens intently when Danio he moves out of sight.

"Something happened in the Pawn Shop?" Toddy asks.

Zem is alerted to the sound of the rear flyscreen opening.

Megan explains the transaction for the gold, omitting the bit where Zem smashed the sign on the glass counter.

Zem hears the noise of a car door opening and closing.

"No one got hurt?" asks Al.

"No. And everyone got paid."

Zem hears the sound of the back door fly screen opening and closing, and then the toilet flushing.

Danio returns to the lounge room, "Later dudes."

Toddy asks him, "We cool?"

"Just keep the suit away from my shop unless I'm there. He's screwed my cash-flow and freaked-out my uncle."

Danio exits and Zem listens to the sound of him walking towards his car. He hears the sound of the car door opening and then closing, the noise as before. Moments later the Torana motor starts up and the car drives away.

Zem is silent, thinking deeply.

"Payday," says Megan. She digs out wads of cash from her pocket and counts out the money onto the table. "Three thousand each, minus commission."

Zem is not paying attention. He is replaying the last few minutes in his head. Protect Megan, Toddy, Al and the tobacco patch. And the bag. The bag. He walks along the hallway to his room and looks under the bed to find that the bag is missing. A blind fury rises in him, and stands, breathing deeply. *What the hell was going on?*

He is disturbed by Toddy saying, "Everything okay, Bro?"

Zem is unable to speak. He is stuck, motionless, staring at the empty space under the bed. Toddy picks up on this. He says, "Your bag's gone."

Zem growls, "This house has inadequate security."

"Its a bush shack, brother," says Toddy, defensively.

"Danio took it."

"Theieving bastard. That's not the first thing he has stolen from me. I'll call him."

"What for?" asks Zem.

"You're right we should just go there."

"Where?"

"Close. Out near the gun club"

"Not now. Later."

"Don't you want to get it back before he empties it?"

"He won't get into the bag."

"Really?"

"Toddy, without that bag I am just a stranger in a suit."

"Sure bro. But..."

"But what?"

"He lives with bikers."

"What are bikers?"

"Angry men who live outside of the law."

"Don't worry about angry men, Toddy. I just need a ride."

"When?"

"Witching hour."

Wasting the Crew

At three in the morning, Toddy looks inside Zem's room to see him sitting on the side of his bed, wating patiently. Together, they slip out the back door to the ute. Toddy instructs Zem to push the car until it is sufficiently far from the house so that the engine noise won't wake Megan or Al.

Toddy drives, saying nothing, feeling tense. The instrument lights in the dashboard illuminate the cabin of the vehicle with a pale green light and Toddy shoots a nervous glance at Zem to see that Zem's eyes are fixed on the road ahead as if nothing else exists in the universe.

Toddy pulls up outside the gate of Danio's house. It is an old Queenslander on a large block. The nearest neighbors are hundreds of meters away. There are hotted-up cars and motorbikes in the front yard. The house is dark.

Toddy turns off the engine and sits silently. He looks to Zem and sees Zem is looking at him. "You want me talk to him?"

"This isn't about talking," says Zem. "Go home."

"What are you going to do?"

"Toddy, you just have to go home."

Zem steps out of the car, into the night. Toddy watches him walk up the dirt driveway towards the house, but he is too tense to start the engine. He sits in the car listening intently. Time ticks by. In the distance, there is the sound of a dog barking. Then the dog goes silent.

Toddy hits the ignition, makes a u-turn and drives away. But he gets only about a hundred meters then stops. He turns off the engine and the lights and sits in the dark.

In the yard, Zem steps over the dead guard dogs, their

necks broken. He approaches the veranda, silently puts his hand on the handle and turns it. The back door is unlocked.

He steps inside the kitchen. It is quiet inside the house and half dark. He stands, listening intently. Then he moves along the hallway to the first room. The door is closed and he places his hand on the doorknob and twists it slowly. He pushes the door open and looks inside. There is a bed from which a fat man sits up rubbing his eyes.

"I'm looking for Danio," says Zem, quietly.

"Next door down. Who are you?"

"Friend."

Zem closes the door quietly behind him. The next door is the same. He opens it quietly. Danio is asleep in his bed. Zem's bag is on the floor. What is the Earth protocol now, Zem wonders, does he just take the bag and leave?

There is a noise behind him. Zem turns to see the fat man step out of his room carrying something. A firearm.

"Danio! Wake up!" shouts the fat man. He raises the shotgun, aiming it in the direction of Zem's head, "Hand's up, f**ker!"

In a seamless movement, Zem steps to one side, clasping his his hands on the shotgun, yanks the weapon from the fat man's hands and slams the butt into his belly, hard. The fat man buckles clutching his gut, groaning. A second blow with the butt on the back of the head sends the man to the floor.

Zem takes a second to investigate the weapon, recognising the type design from his training. *Shotgun. Pump action. Safety off. Trigger.*

There is a commotion in Danio's room. Zem pushes open the door. The bedside light is on. Danio coming at him wearing just undies. Zem fires. *BOOM!* Cartridge discharge into chest at close range. Danio down taking the bedside lamp down with him. The blood looks black in the half-light. Zem cocks the weapon by sliding back the action.

Zem turns his attention to the next room along the hallway. An automatic weapon opens fire throwing bullets through the wall. There is a pattern to the bullet holes. Zem shoots through the wall. A scream. Zem reloads. Kicks open the door. A woman is holding her bleeding wrist. A man next is trying to push a magazine into a machine pistol. *BOOM!* Reload. *BOOM!*

A groan from the hallway. The fat man is trying to rise. Zem pushes the barrel against his neck. *BOOM!*

Zem reloeads. He becomes motionless. Standing there in the hallway, listening intently. It is quiet. *Is this Earth*, he wonders. *Is this what it's like?*

He scouts the the house to finds that he is alone with four dead humans and the dead dogs in the yard. He returns to Danio's room and retrieves his bag. Then he locates Danio's trousers and fossicks in the pockets and retrieves the three gold nuggets.

In the kitchen, Zem stops and thinks hard. Then, with the gun and his bag he steps out of the house. He holds the gun by his side and walks along the road, the way he came in.

The ute is there with Toddy sitting inside. He walks past it, cursing quietly. Toddy watches him, uncertain but Zem keeps walking. Toddy fires the engine, pulls up alongside. Toddy winds down the window.

"Get in the car, dude."

"Go home, Toddy!" Zem barks. "Go! Go! Go!"

Toddy sees the look on Zem's face and feels a chill sweep up his spine. He drives away into the dark.

Zem watches the taillights of the car fade into the distance, and he looks around. Then he moves away from the road into the forest and disappears into the night.

Penthouse Proposal

Next morning, Zem is eating dippy eggs with Megan and Al at the kitchen bench when Toddy wanders into the lounge.

"Hey, Toddy. Want some dippy eggs," asks Megan.

"Whatever."

"That's code for yes," Megan tells Zem. She says, "Hey Toddy, did you move the car last night?"

"Don't know anything about it."

"Maybe Al is right. Ute fairies."

Toddy catches Zem's eye, "You got a minute?" he asks. He ushers Zem step outside and closes the fly screen door behind them.

"You got your bag?" Toddy asks.

"Sure."

"Want to tell me what happened?"

"Do you know what plausible deniability is?" asks Zem.

Toddy thinks about this for a while then says, "I am innocent because I don't know?"

"My eggs are getting cold," Zem returns to the kitchen.

After a few moments Toddy joins him, "Definitely ute fairies," he tells Megan.

"So I have a crazy idea I want to pitch," says Megan putting toast next to the eggs on Toddy's plate. "Toddy, are you listening?"

"Whatever."

"After shopping the other day, Zem and I had a little Townsville adventure. You know the units overlooking the marina near the Strand? Well, we checked out this penthouse. Five rooms, all with ensuites."

"It has excellent security," says Zem.

"Penthouse? Awesome," says Al.

"I was thinking we could live there," says Megan.

Toddy looks up, stunned. "No!" he says, instinctively.

"Zem has offered to pay a year's rent upfront, plus money for bills and a cleaner. He regards that as fair exchange for us just being around for him."

Toddy rests back in his chair. He sees that he is the last one to know, as Megan has clearly already gained Al's consent. He pushes his plate away and walks out the back door and slams the fly screen.

"I think it's an awesome idea," says Al. "Maybe we could get a car with more than three seats."

"We could do that," says Zem.

"Do you want to go talk to him," asks Megan.

Zem walks along the corridor, out the back door, along the track to where Toddy is sitting on a tree stump next to the chop-chop patch. The solar panels are working, and a fine mist of water fills the air.

Toddy looks up at Zem, feeling overwhelmed by the strength projected by the clothes and his strong physique.

"Is everything okay?" asks Zem.

"You know what, man? Four days ago everything was just sweet. I got this pad. I got my crop. Hanging with Megan and Al. Sure, the irrigation didn't work, but it was rain-fed, you know. Then some space freak pops into existence in front of me and next thing I don't need to grow chop-chop because three grand just turned up. And I don't even want to know what you did last night. But it's going to blow back."

"Was he your friend?"

"No. He was just a fat jerk who bought my chop-chop and

stole shit from me.,"

"What is this stuff anyway?" asked Zem turning his attention to the tobacco plants.

"You don't get it do you?" Toddy steps from his tree stump and draws one of the leaves towards him. "This is chop-chop," he says. "Organically grown tobacco, irrigated with solar powered irrigation, thanks to you. No pesticides or poisons. No big ugly corporations or slave labour."

"Why don't you clear these trees and plant some more?" suggests Zem, indicating towards the forest.

"Zem, you know nothing about contraband. It's supposed to be small scale. If it is any larger the coppers will be onto us, big time."

"Coppers?"

"I don't know about this Penthouse idea, Zem. But I don't know about this bush shack anymore, either."

"Why don't you takeTake a look at the apartment," suggests Zem.

"Not today, Zem. I'm still freaked out about last night." Toddy approaches Zem, touches the lapel of his silk shirt, with a malicious smile, "I have an idea."

"What's that."

"I am going to smoke you up and get you smashed."

Toddy walks into the lounge room and announces, "Cancel all your plans. We've got a new one."

Megan smiles approvingly at Toddy's changed demeanour.

"Al, get the stash. Megan, how much beer have we got? She checks the fridge, "About a carton."

"Good. I reckon it's time we got old mate Zem smashedbent."

"Noice," says Al, pulling a bag of cannabis buds from

under his seat cushion.

"What about the apartment?" asks Megan.

"Get wasted today," says Toddy. "~~PVisit p~~enthouse tomorrow."

The Session

Santana is playing on the stereo. The coffee table is cleared, the ashtray emptied. Zem, Toddy, Megan and Al are in their normal seats. Al is delicately licking cigarette papers.

Megan sits with her legs tucked up under her body, leafing through one of Zem's documents, *Humanity: Progress to Date*. "So, there is now eight billion humans on Earth," she says.

"Hey," says Al. "Imagine if you could invent something that everybody wanted and make a dollar each off them. You'd have like eight billion dollars."

"What did you have in mind?" asks Zem, genuinely interested in the ordered goings on around the coffee table.

"I don't know," says Al. "A branded fork, maybe."

"Chinese don't use forks," says Megan. "That's a quarter of your market gone."

"Chopsticks then."

"It's the same problem," says Toddy. "You need something that is a common need for all humans."

"Hairbrush," says Al.

"Bald people," says Toddy.

"Toilet paper," says Megan, and they all laugh.

"Toilet paper is good," says Al. "Let's say the roll lasts a week, that's eight billion a week. Imagine that."

Megan continues reading, "It says here that most of the world's population doesn't have a flushing toilet. Or electricity. And a third can't even secure protection from the elements. That's so depressing."

"That's screwed my business plan," says Al.

"Read us something cheery, Megan."

"*Shhh*," says Toddy. "Do you hear that?" In the distance is the sound of motorcycles engines approaching. Toddy stands, looks out the window and gasps, "Oh, bugger."

Two Harley Davidson motorcycles pull up outside. The noise of their engines has Zem alert.

"Who's that?" asks Megan.

"Danio's cousin," says Toddy, then to Zem, "Yo! Spaceman. Go wait in your room. I'm serious brother. Move." Toddy claps his hands for effect.

"I can protect you," says Zem.

"Just go," snaps Megan.

Zem does as requested. He sits on the bed with the ajar enough that he can hear the conversation from the lounge room.

A stocky man with a wispy beard and colours enters the living room followed by a tall gaunt man with bad skin. Both wear stained jeans, black motorcycle tee shirts, and black vests.

The stocky man looks distraught. He remains standing to tell his story. "Hi Toddy, Al, Megs," he says.

"Hey, Sid, Mike," says Toddy. "Come in bro. Sit down."

"I'm all good. Did you hear about Danio and the crew?"

Hairs come up on Toddy's forearm, "No mate, what happened?"

"Someone wasted them last night. All of them. They shot Dingo in the back of the head. They killed his f**king dogs, man. Danio's shot in the chest. Maria is dead. And Blake."

"Whoa!" says Toddy, covering his mouth.

"Are the police there?" asks Al.

"Police? F**k me! It's like Crime Scene Miami comes to Townsville. State police. Federal police. Dogs. Choppers in the air. All the news media outside."

"How did you find out?" asks Toddy.

Sid indicates towards Mike, the skinny man standing behind him. "Mike's brother works with the cops. Know anything about it Toddy? I talked to Danio last night. He says he was over here. Says something about Megs and some dude sold some gold to his uncle?"

Toddy says, "Danio was here last night. He didn't say anything odd."

"So who is the dude with Megs?" asks Sid.

"He's my Uncle," says Megan, quickly, "From Melbourne."

"Danio says he was dressed like a scruff. Wearing that shirt." Sid points to the Swivel Bitch t-shirt that Toddy is wearing.

"Washing day," says Al. "He borrowed some clothes."

"Do the coppers know who did it?" asks Toddy.

"Cairns mob, they reckon. There was some blue over a deal went bad in Cardwell. We're getting out of town. Really suggest you do likewise, Toddy."

"Why would I leave town? I'm just a grower."

"Coppers mate. They found some of your chop-chop. If they connect the tobacco to your patch, then they'll want to talk to you. Help them with their enquiries, whatever."

"Oh, man," says Toddy, despondently.

"We've gotta go," says Sid. "Going to Airlie for a few weeks. If you hear anything, call me, okay."

"Yes, mate," says Toddy.

"And Toddy," says Sid. "Serious. Get out of here. Just go somewhere else."

Sid and Mike depart. They noisily start their bikes, rev the engines for a while, and then drive away.

When the engine noise had passed, Toddy leans back in his

seat and exhales deeply, "Oh, man. That scared the shit out of me."

"Where are you going?" asks Toddy watching Megan ~~rise~~.

"I am going to talk to Zem."

"Sit down, Megan~~,~~" Toddy says, forcefully. "I'll get him."

Megan faces Toddy and projects the message: *sort this shit out, or I will.*

Toddy enters Zem's room and closes the door ~~behind him~~.

"Don't get up, space assassin. Time for a chat."

Zem settles himself back on his bed and looks up at Toddy, impassively. Toddy paces back and forth ~~for a time~~, forming his words.

"You know, Zem. Next time you decide to waste a crew, how about you just, like... ~~Like~~ don't."

Zem looks at the floor, silently.

"Your killing spree is now in my house. You know anything about forensics? You know what that is?"

"What is it?"

"It's the science of finding out who wasted Danio and his mates so they can send him and his accomplices to prison for life. You leave any hairs behind, Zem? Footprints? Fingerprints? Did you spit in anyone's face and leave your DNA?"

Zem looks at the floor, shaking his head.

Toddy grunts. He wipes his hand over his face. "Well, if we are lucky only you and I know the truth and the cops won't have any reason to come here."

"I am sorry," says Zem. He feels vulnerable and conflicted.

"Whatever. Listen, next time you decide you want to blow four scumbags away, tell me about it. Maybe there is a verbal solution. Okay?"

Toddy watches Zem nodding, then he leaves the room.
After a few minutes, Zem follows him, and takes his place on
the couch. He looks up to see that Megan has her eyes fixed
on his and a scowl on her face.

"Zem," she says curtly. "Look at me. Simple yes or no
answer. Do you know anything about what happened to
Danio and his mates last night?"

Zem feels Toddy tap his foot and sees Toddy making the
slightest head shaking movement.

"Last night," Zem says to Megan, "I was dreaming."

Toddy exhales a long, quiet sigh. He picks up one of the
rolled-up cigarettes and ignites a lighter. He pauses for a
long beat, staring at the orange flame. Then he puts the rollie
back on the table.

"Okay," he says. "Let's go check out the penthouse."

Animal, Mineral, Vegetable

A month later, Zem, Toddy, Megan and Al have settled into the Penthouse and a routine has emerged. Zem has sold more of his gold and one of the crystals, and this has provided sufficient cash to pay the rent, and shout buy everyone clothes and toys and whatever they wanted.

Al has connected the largest flat screen TV he could find to a cable network. Megan has purchased a second-hand car. Toddy has been treated to the largest of the rooms in the apartment, and he has taken to the new lifestyle. He has kept his appearance smart, and focused on his studies and put his contraband on the backburner.

During the day, Megan drives Toddy and Al to university while Zem stays in his quarters that now look more like NASA mission control than a bedroom. On his workstation is the latest Apple computer connected with two extra monitors and broadband internet. The colour printer runs hot with documents that he finds through endless hours of browsing the web. Zem prints them, reads them, and ruminates about them, trying to piece it all together.

In the evenings, Megan drives the boys home, and they argue about which take away venue should provide that night's food. Megan rings for it, Al sets the table, and Toddy goes downstairs and retrieves the food when it arrives at the security gate.

The weeks come and go, and a long weekend breaks the routine. The four sit around the glass table on the balcony overlooking the marina.

Toddy lights a rollie from his bag of chop-chop and blows blue smoke in the air. "So where were we?" he asks.

"Selling toilet rolls to everyone on the planet," says Al.

"Not going to work," says Megan. "Not everyone wipes their ass." Everyone laughs.

"We'll sell them finger soap," says Al.

"That's two products then," says Toddy. "I don't think there is any one thing that connects humans together. Apart from water, and that is free."

"So what you been reading today, Zem?" asks Al.

"Yeah," Zem says contemplatively. "I want to show you something." He visits his room and returns to the balcony with his bag and places it on the table. "I think we should have a conversation about this bag."

Zem passes the pouch to Toddy, "~~See if you can o~~Open ~~it it~~."

"This is a cool trick~~so cool, this trick~~," says Megan. She snuggles up in her chair and watches Toddy fumble.

He examines the bag, rotating it in his hands, looking for an opening. He squeezes it, shakes it, and puts his ear to it. After fifty seconds he grunts and hands the bag to Al.

Al's investigation is much more thorough. He turns, twists, and examines the pouch in the light. He takes a knife and scrapes the material, checking for wear. Al's investigations are so focused that his wrestle with the bag becomes part of the furniture, and the conversation proceeds without him. Eventually, he surfaces with a grunt and offers the bag to Megan.

"It's already beat me~~Oh, no~~," she says, waving it away. ~~"It's already beat me."~~

Al hands the bag to Zem who says, "The pattern indicates which way is up."

"What pattern?" Toddy challenges him.

"This pattern," says Zem. He rotates the bag, and it instantly falls open in his hands.

Al nearly falls off his seat. "That is…" says Al, but he is unable to complete his sentence.

"It likes me," says Zem.

"Do we get to see what's inside," asks Megan.

"Absolutely. Let's clear the table."

"Shit, yeah," says Al. He starts moving items onto the floor. Megan retrieves a cloth from the kitchen and wipes down the glass. Within a few minutes, the surface clean and Zem empties out the contents of the bag in front of him. He arranges the pieces into separate groups and then moves them into the center of the table, one by one.

First, he slides forward the remaining gold nuggets. "So, we have the gold nuggets. These, plus the ones I sold to pay the rent," says Zem.

"And the three at the Pawn Shop," says Megan.

"I got those ba__," says Zem, but stops just in time. He grits his teeth and holds his breath, hoping that Megan hasn't picked up on his revelation. He grimaces, feeling an emotion that he has felt numerous times since being on Earth: *inadvertent self-sabotage.*

"And this," he continues, feeling light-headed as he slides a metal block across the table. "I don't know what this is. And these," he holds up the two glass vials, one containing the green powder, the other the brown liquid. He hands the vials to Toddy who gives them short shrift.

"Spirulina and crude oil," says Toddy. "It's obvious."

"And I have no idea what this is for," says Zem sliding an electronic device across the glass table. The device is made of lightweight, gray grey metal. It has three separate parts

61

connected with swivels, and recesses that look like they would fit fingertips.

Al reaches for the device and studies it. "Wow. It looks like a remote control on crystal meth." He fiddles with the device and finds that each segment moves independently to its adjoining piece and that there are dozens of different configurations.

"And these," says Zem, handing the gemstone to Megan and the container containing the crystals to Toddy.

"Silica," says Toddy. "Simple. It goes like this." He arranges the crude oil, spirulina, and silica in a row in front of him. "Animal. Vegetable. Mineral. It's obvious."

"Toddy, you just jump to conclusions and don't want to jump off them," says Al.

"This is like one of those mad gemstones that the Russian monarchs used to own," says Megan examining the jewel.

"Help me out guys," says Zem, despondently. "I spend my days obsessively researching things. My head is full of global finance, politics, energy networks. I feel as though I should be doing something. And all of these things are a part of it."

"I think I'm onto it," says Al studying the electronic device. He stands, moves towards the door, "I am going to check it in the light."

Megan watches Al walk inside. She places her hand on Zem's wrist, comfortingly, "It's okay Zem. We'll get you through it."

"I don't know where I'd be without you guys," says Zem, honestly. "Probably wandering around the bush at Alligator Creek, eating wallabies."

Zem is cut off by an excited noise from the lounge room. Al has made a discovery with the remote control, "Hey, check it out!"

Zem enters the lounge room followed by Megan and Toddy.

"How cool is this?" Al says, holding up the device. "I was just twisting it around and it lit up. Like it's switched on or something."

Zem sits next to Al and takes the device, observing the shape that it has formed. He turns it around in his hands, observing the lights twinkling. Then he recognizes a pattern.

"Look, hold it like this," says Al, adjusting it in Zem's hands. "See, these little indentations are for your fingers. Try it."

Zem positions the device as Al had suggested. He places his fingertips in the recesses, but nothing happens. Zem stands, looking at the device in his hands, intrigued. He paces around the lounge room as his Earth friends watch him, enthralled.

"Try something else, says Megan. "Maybe squeeze it."

Zem looks at her, then back to the device. He adjusts its position in his hand slightly, and squeezes his fingertips into the recesses.

Suddenly, a bolt of electricity shoots up Zem's arm as a booming noise like a gunshot - *CRACK!* – and a brilliant flash of bright blue light.

"Ow!" Zem drops the device on the floor, jumping back in shock.

The apartment is plunged into darkness as the lights shut off.

"How cool is that," says Toddy.

"Did you see that?" asks Zem. "Did you see her?"

"Her?" asks Megan. "What?"

"What happened to the lights?" asks Al.

"Check the switchboard in the pantry," says Toddy. "The safety has probably flicked off."

"Did you see someone?" asks Megan. "The woman from your dream?"

"What woman?" asks Toddy.

"You remember when Zem first arrived and freaked us out in the kitchen and it turns out he was dreaming about some woman," says Megan.

"Was that before or after he spewed googy egg on me?"

"Just before, I think," says Megan.

Al rummages around in the pantry and finds that the safety circuits are in the 'off' position. He turns them all on and the apartment illuminates as before. He returns to the lounge room and sees the lights blinking on the cable TV box, "Oh, man, I'm going to have to reset the cable."

"What caused that?" asks Megan.

"Electromagnetic pulse, maybe," say Al. "You get them with nuclear explosions. You didn't just set off a nuke, did you Zem?"

"I don't think so," says Zem, examining the remote control in his hand.

"Anyway, lights are back on. You want to see if we can do it again?" says Al, enthusiastically.

"Again?" says Zem.

"Where was the woman?" asks Megan.

"Just up in front of me," says Zem indicating with his hands.

"Well, assuming she comes back and she sticks around, I'd like to see her," says Megan. "So why don't you stand there, face that way, press the thing, and don't drop it this time."

"Shit yeah," says Al, taking a seat on the couch between Megan and Toddy. "Who needs cable when we've got Zem's hot chick on the big screen."

"Hold up," says Toddy, I need a beer. Anyone else?"

"I'll have one," says Al.

"Me too," says Megan. "None for Zem while he's talking to his girlfriend, though."

"She's hardly my girlfriend, Megan. She's like three hundred years old."

"Cosmic Cougar," says Al and they all laugh.

Toddy returns with the beers and hands them out.

Then Toddy, Al and Megan sit in the plush comfy chairs in the penthouse that overlooks the Townsville Marina. Zem stands with his back to them holding the electronic device that looks like a remote control on crystal meth.

"Okay," says Toddy, theatrically. "And; action!"

Zem glances at his three Earth friends, feeling both anxious and excited. Maybe today he finds out what it's all about. He turns back to the empty wall and squeezes his fingertips into the ~~remote control~~remote-control device.

Music Unimpressed

CRACK!! A bright blue flash of light. A bolt of electricity shoots up Zem's arm, but he fights against it and keeps tight hold of the device. The air thickens as blue, translucent bubbles form all around him. The bubbles expand, filling the whole room. Lightning sparks between the bubbles.

Toddy, Al and Megan are dumbstruck watching the apartment fill with swirling blue balls, obscuring everything, like -smoke a nightclub dance floor. The room fills with blue bubbles.

"This is like when he first arrived," says Al.

The bubbles expand and multiply and when they seem to be at their peak, the pop and disappear, and in their place is a elder woman. *A most extraordinary woman.*

She wears a nautilus shell on her head and has gold braid in her hair. Covering her shoulders is a material that looks like fine moss. She looks old but lively and healthy.

She focuses on Zem, who is standing, bolt upright, trembling. Her facial expression indicates that she knows Zem and that she is both surprised and shocked to see him. She sighs, audibly, as though greatly relieved to see him. And then her attention turns to the Zem's three human companions, welded to their seats, their eyes wide open.

The woman's face softens, showing something between a concerned frown and empathy, "Zemitheree," she says, speaking in a language that only Zem can understand. "Thank Palau you are safe. Where are you?"

"*Ummm.* Do I know you?" asks Zem.

"Oh, Zemitheree. Are you safe? Do you have security?"

"I am safe with friends. Who are you?"

"You know well who I am. But you've not been taking Virid."

"Virid?" asks Zem.

"Hold on, I want Verten to see you."

A moment later a man appears. He is old, exquisitely dressed.

"Zemitheree! Thank Palau you are alive. Are you sick?"

"Who are you?" asks Zem.

"He hasn't been taking his Virid," says Music.

"There is no point having this conversation, then," says Verten, dismissively.

"Who are you people?" protests Zem, "Who am I?"

Music suddenly becomes very stern. She fixes Zem with a hard stare, "Listen to me, Zemitheree. Listen very carefully! You cannot understand the gravitas of what will unfold on this planet if you do not follow these instructions to their letter. Do I have your attention?"

"You know my name."

"I have known your name for a very long time. Inside your transit pouch is a green powder. Do you still have this?"

"Please say yes," says Verten.

"I have it," says Zem.

Music continues, "This is what you must do. Obtain a clear container and fill it with clean rainwater. Put a sprinkle of the green powder into the water and leave it in the sun for a full day. Do you understand?"

"Why would I do this?"

Verten snarls, "You cannot possibly understand who you are or what you are supposed to do unless you drink the Virid."

Music says, "Drink three liters the first day, and then a

litre every day after. Every day. Keep topping up the
container with rain-water."

"What is this for?" asks Zem.

"It will help you transcend your Hominid limitations.
Connect you with your Parrathean capabilities and memories.
Under no circumstance must the Earth people be allowed to
drink the Virid. We cannot allow that gene pool to have
transcendent abilities. Do you understand me?"

"Well, yes, I guess," says Zem, noncommittally.

"Do you understand me!?"

"Yes."

"Zemitheree, the space link we are speaking over will not
last long. You must go now. Do as we say. Communicate
with us in the same manner in one week. I will explain your
mission then."

Zem is breathless. He looks from Music to Verten,
"Okay."

"Then let go of the Space Link," says Music. "Do it now."

Zem looks down at the device in his hands, the Space Link.
He lets it fall to the floor. Instantly Music and Verten
disappear and he is standing in the darkened apartment.

Zem stands motionless, trying to piece all this new
information together. Then he turns slowly to see Megan,
Toddy and Al on the couch. "Are you okay," he asks,
concerned to see his three friends motionless, silently
blinking, their beers still full.

Toddy says, "If that was your parents, you are so in the
shit."

"Did you see that?" asks Zem.

"Saw everything," says Al. "Didn't understand it though,
you were all talking in some foreign language."

Zem kneels on the floor, exhausted.

"Did they tell you why you are here?" asks Megan.

"They wouldn't tell me. They said I wouldn't understand."

"What did they say, they were talking enough?" says Toddy.

"They said I need to get a big glass jar and fill it with rainwater. Can you help me with that?"

Brewing Virid

As it happens, Al knows a guy who sells rainwater. He arrived the following day with a twenty-liter drum. Megan finds a small fish tank for sale at the university, and sets it up on the balcony.

Once the tank is thoroughly scrubbed and filled with rainwater, Zem opens the glass vial and adds a sprinkle of green powder onto the water surface. They all peer into the tank as the powder dissolves, turning the water a pale green colour.

"What happens now?" asks Toddy.

"We wait a day," says Zem.

The following day, the water in the fish tank is dark green and viscous. Megan retrieves a measuring container from the kitchen and glasses. She measures out a liter and pours three glasses full of Virid. Toddy, Al and Zem watch her as she works, Zem wearing the look of a condemned man.

"Okay," she says to Zem. "This is the first three of nine glasses. You ready?"

Zem looks apprehensively at the dark green liquid. He picks up the first glass and sniffs it.

"How is it?" Megan asks.

"Fruity," says Zem. "In a bad way."

Al picks up a glass and sniffs, "Whoa! Its like a seaweed milkshake."

"I don't think you guys should try this," says Zem, remembering his instructions not to let humans drink the Virid. He brings the glass to his mouth, then commits and swallows it in one gulp.

Oh, Yuk!

Zem screws up his face, wiping his mouth on the sleeve of his silk shirt. "Wow. That's heavy."

"One down," says Toddy, chuckling cruelly, "Eight to go."

Megan refills the measuring container and tops up the first glass. Zem prepares himself then gulps down glass two. Then glass three. Megan dutifully refills after him.

After the fifth glass, Zem calls a halt, "How much is that?" he asks, queasily.

"Five. Over half-way," says Al. "You okay?"

"I think so," says Zem, obviously pained. "I might sit this out for a bit, though."

After a few minutes ruminating on his fate, Zem beckons for the sixth glass. It is a struggle. The seventh and eight are worse. He takes a full ten minutes to down the ninth and final glass.

"He's done it," says Megan proudly. She goes to the kitchen and washes out the measuring container. Then she encourages Toddy to help her refill the fish tank with rainwater. When they are finished, they sit down with Zem and observe him. He is looking decidedly full.

"I think I might take a lie down," he says. Megan escorts him to the couch and he settles himself, with one arm across his face and the other on his belly.

Megan returns to the table on the balcony where Toddy and Al are smoking rollies.

"I think he will be okay," she says.

"What do you reckon that stuff is?" asks Al.

"Don't know," says Toddy. "Alien food."

"I wonder if it will change his behavior?" says Megan.

"He can't get any weirder," says Al.

Later that night, Zem is still lying on the couch. He is

awake, staring at the ceiling. Megan sits next to him and takes his hand, "How are you feeling?"

"Good actually, refreshed, in fact."

"You were brave today. Three litres deserves a medal."

"I think you are right."

"Well, good night brave spaceman, see you in the morning." Megan leans down and places a small kiss on his forehead.

"Goodnight Megan. Thanks for your support." Zem watches as she moves out of the lounge towards her room.

At 3 a.m. Zem is wide-awake and seated at the table on the veranda reading one of his reports. He hears the noise of a text message being received in one of the rooms. A few minutes later he watches as Megan moves from her room into Toddy's, wearing a nightie.

Twenty minutes later, Megan steps into the hallway. She sees Zem on the balcony and pauses a while to observe him. He has a pile of documents next to him and is speed-reading, giving each two-page spread about thirty seconds of attention before he flicks over to the next.

"Hey, Zem. You're up late."

He doesn't hear her at first, so she moves closer, "Zemmy?"

Zem looks up with a start. "Hey, Megan. You are up late."

She looks at the floor and makes a quiet chuckle, "Booty call," she says with a wry smile. "What are you reading?"

"It's a report on global wealth distribution."

"Did that Virid stuff have any effect?"

"Sort of. I feel like I have more clarity. Still don't know what I am looking at though."

"Don't stay up too late. I'm going to bed."

"Night, Megan."

Later, at 10 a.m. and Megan steps out of her room again and makes for the kitchen. She is standing by the kettle waiting for it to boil when she notices that Zem is still in his chair reading through documents. He has a laptop and a pile of printed documents. In his room, a printer is running hot, spitting out a long stream of pages. Megan notices the odd way that Zem is reading the documents: a total immersion in speed reading.

"Hi Zem," she says.

Zem doesn't break from his pace. She watches as his eyes zoom around the figures and tables and diagrams in the document. Less a set of eyes, more like industrial lasers.

"Zem," she says, but no reply, just the robot scanner.

Toddy wanders out onto the balcony, yawning. He stretches, scratches his belly then sees the look on Megan's face.

Toddy leans in, looks closely at Zem's laser eyes, slaps his hand on the table and shouts, "Yo! Zem!"

Zem snaps out violently. "Whoa!" The document flies from his hands and he leaps to his feet making a sharp, adrenalin-fired grunt. He lands in a defensive position, his eyes darting back and forth looking for danger. His chest is pounding, air shifting rapidly in and out of his lungs.

"Where were you?" asks Megan, her face red, almost in tears.

"Looks like he's on speed," says Toddy.

"Where am I?" asks Zem, anxiously.

"You're on the balcony, dude," shouts Toddy. "What is this shit you are reading anyway?" Toddy retrieves the document from the floor: *Advances in Nuclear Fusion Technology*.

"You really need to lighten up, Zem. Try the Townsville Bulletin. You alright Megan?"

"I thought we had lost him."

Zem is calmer now, but bewildered. He looks at the documents piled around his feet, sheepishly. His head is pounding with words, diagrams, concepts and data. He looks out across the marina and feels the familiarity of his surroundings return, comfortingly.

"I am okay now. Just got a bit caught up," he says, quietly.

"Sucked in, more like," says Toddy.

"Do you want some breakfast?" asks Megan.

"No," says Zem.

"No?"

"I mean no, thanks."

"I mean, why don't you want any breakfast? You normally eat like a horse."

Zem looks nonplussed. How does he eat like a horse? What is it with these humans constantly forcing food onto each other? Zem glances at the tank full of Virid. That's all he wants.

Mission Disclosure

Days pass and Zem has had no appetite for either food or sleep since he first drank the Virid. Despite this, he feels healthy and robust and all he wants to do is read and research.

He makes a conscious effort to drag himself away from his documents when Megan and Al and Toddy are around because he still feels as though he needs them close. However, now he finds the conversations around the table on the balcony exceptionally dull. He doesn't want to talk about pygmies or what to sell everyone on the planet.

When his friends turn in for the night, Zem restarts his research. His printer runs hot, silenced by a blanket. He tries to maintain the impression that he is sleeping regular hours, but his not eating can't be hidden.

A week passes and Zem announces that he is going to place a call on the remote-control device. Initially, he wants to make the call alone, but his three friends browbeat him into having an audience. He feels that he owes them this insight into his life, even if they are unable to decipher the words.

Megan, Al, and Toddy resume their places on the sofa and, as before, Zem stands with his back to them and activates the device. There is a loud *CRACK!*, a blue flash and the lights fail. The lounge fills with blue bubbles.

The bubbles fade and Music appears promptly. Her face breaks into a big smile when she lays eyes on him, "Zemitheree," she coos. "You have been taking your Virid. I'm bringing in the Committee."

Then Music notices Megan and Al and Toddy sitting in the

couch each with a freshly opened beer in their hands. Music's face changes immediately, the tone of her voice is unmistakable.

"Zemitheree," she barks. "What are those humans doing here? This cannot be permitted."

"These are my friends."

"Your friends?" she laughs, coarsely. "You weren't sent to Earth to make friends. Send them away."

"They can't understand you, so why be concerned?" argues Zem. Verten appears, and then a dozen old faces, floating in mid-air.

Verten says, "He has his pets with him again."

"Be nice, Verten, they are hominids, like us," says Music.

"How are you Zemitheree?" asks Verten. "Seeing things clearly now?"

"Crystal clear, but I don't know what I am looking at."

Music turns to the Parrathean elders behind her. Like her, they wear prosthetic adornments and are very old, but healthy looking.

Music tells them, "You can see the agent is well, but clearly we have lost some time due to the nature of his arrival on Earth. I will brief you again when there is significant progress. Until then, be gone."

The Committee members fade from view. Music turns her attention to Zemitheree.

"Zemitheree, it may have come to your attention that you are on Earth for a very important reason. I trust that the Virid has worked had its desired effect and that you are now ready to begin."

"I have been ready since the day I arrived," says Zem.

"Then listen up, Zemitheree Beden-ifictu," says Music,

looking at him directly. "This is your mission."

Underworld Contacts

The next day, once Megan, Al and Toddy are out of the house, Zem exits the apartment and walks into town. As he walks, he thinks through what Music has told him, mapping out a plan.

Zem walks around the city center until he comes to a seedy bar. He doesn't find what he is looking for there, so he walks on to the next. Eventually, he comes to a hotel outside of which are parked six Harley Davidson motorcycles.

He moves towards the motorcycles. In his suit, tie and shiny shoes, Zem looks distinctly out of place next to the bikes. Then he waits.

It is not long before he draws the attention of one of the bikers who steps out from the bar. Three other men watch on. Stovepipe has a face scarred with acne pockmarks. He wears leathers with no shirt revealing tufts of curly hair on his chest. He has black jeans and boots with chains. His blue reflective sunglasses seal perfectly against his face, making him look more like an insect than a human. He moves into Zem's space and stands there, their noses close together. Zem looks into the insect eyes, ready to slam heads in a moment's notice.

Zem says calmly, "I need to talk to your boss."

Stovepipe snorts. He looks Zem up and down then returns to the tavern with his shabby entourage. Zem follows them inside and takes a stool at the bar observing them. At first Stovepipe just looks at him. Eventually, he takes out a mobile phone, dials, talks secretively into it and then addresses Zem.

"What do you want?" asks Stovepipe.

"I know what happened to Danio," says Zem.

Stovepipe steps off his stool and walks a few paces away and talks into the phone, all the time observing Zem. Finally, he closes the handset and moves back to the bar. He skulls the remainder of his drink.

"Alright boys," says Stovepipe and his men finish up their drinks. Stovepipe points to the door and ushers Zem outside.

The bikers step onto their Harleys and Zem is handed a faceless, black helmet. Then Stovepipe nods to one of his crew who beckons for Zem to sit on the pillion seat, behind him. The bikers rev up loudly, then depart.

They ride for forty minutes, heading north out of Townsville, past the industrial estate and along the Bruce Highway. The bikers turn into the grounds of an old brick factory and once inside they drive in slow circles around a ruined building, killing time.

Eventually, another five bikes pull up under the rusty tin roof of the factory, forming a circle around a structure in the center of the building. Stovepipe leads his riders into the building, with Zem still riding pillion, and they pull up their bikes to complete a circle.

In the center of the circle, is Tarp, the gang leader. He is biggest by far and he moves with a slow purposefulness. There is a ruined brick structure in the center of the ring of bikes and this forms a crude throne. Tarp rests there watching impassively as his men dismount.

Zem removes his helmet and steps into the middle of the circle. He casts his eyes around the group of men. One he recognizes, the old man from the pawn shop who is pointing his nicotine-stained finger. "That's him. That's Mister Nugget."

Tarp steps off his brick throne and approaches Zem. He

runs his fingers over the fabric of Zem's suit, nodding appreciatively.

"So that's how it is done, huh?"

"That's how it's done."

"What do you actually want, you strange man?" asks Tarp.

"I need a new identity."

"Does your present identity have a name?"

"It's called Zem."

"And what is wrong with that one?"

"It's not big enough."

"Well, maybe you're not big enough," says Tarp.

"Oh, I'm plenty big," says Zem. "Bigger than you."

Tarp starts laughing. "Really? You see, I'm actually quite big. And bad. And there are twelve of me."

"I count eleven."

"My numbering ain't good. But I'm a dab hand at mugging. And stabbing. And stomping."

"Well here's a thing," says Zem. "I don't trade with my enemies. So if you want to fight, let's get it on. Otherwise, let's do business."

"*Uh-huh*? So what are you trading?"

"I'll tell you what happened to Danio and his crew."

"There's a start."

"I executed them because Danio stole from me."

Tarp is silent, motionless, staring at Zem. From all around comes a murmur of discontent from his crew. He glances around to see who is doing the moaning.

"Some people here lost family that night," Tarp says.

"Collateral damage," replies Zem, flatly.

"Collateral?" laughs Tarp. "Really?"

"Time has moved on from that concern."

"In this town, collateral damage has a price."

"What price."

"Saying sorry. Penance. Punishment. All of the above."

"Which one is quicker?"

"Saying sorry is the fastest," says Tarp.

"Sorry," says Zem, flatly. "Can we get to the good bit?"

"All good," says Tarp, clapping his hands together. "Moving right on to commerce."

The old boy from the pawn shop starts shouting, "That was my nephew, you can't let him off!"

"Shut your pie-hole, or I shut it for ya!" bellows Tarp turning to face his men. The old man shuffles back to his spot, mumbling to himself.

Tarp looks at his motley crew and barks, "Danio and his crew are dead, ~~and~~ Zem killed them, and he said sorry. That's the story. Now, we could bash right now till he's dead which would be a lot of fun, but I think he might be good for something." Tarp listens for a protest but there are none.

"So, Zem," he says. "What are you good for?"

"I'm weak now,~~," he says.~~ When I'm strong, I may need you."

"You *may* need us?" Tarp laughs.

~~"That's right."~~

"Well ain't you a cheeky little f**king bandicoot," says Tarp. ~~"All this for that."~~

"That's my offer," says Zem.

Tarp thinks it through, rubbing his chin. "Well we don't do identities here, Mister Zem. But I know a guy who knows a guy. So why don't you ~~accept~~ take a ride home and we'll let you know when we are ready to talk again."

Police Visit

Later that evening, Zem arrives back at the apartment. He opens the front door and immediately halts, the hairs coming up on the back of his neck. There are voices coming from inside the apartment. Unfamiliar voices; the authoritative voices of men.

He moves cautiously into the apartment and first sees Toddy and Al standing with their heads lowered. A few more paces inside the apartment Zem sees two uniformed men with side arms, the Queensland state police.

Zem catches Megan's eye, she is in the kitchen resting against the counter.

Megan says, "Hi Zem."

"Is everything okay?" he asks.

"The police were asking if we knew anything about what happened with Danio, the guy who was killed a while ago."

"Where were you that night?" asks one of the officers.

"I was dreaming," says Zem.

Zem moves into the kitchen and rests against the bench next to Megan. Tough men with guns do not worry him. But he knows that there is a cultural finesse that reduces that chance of policemen asking difficult questions.

"You are the Uncle?" asks one of the policemen.

"Yes," says Megan.

"He can answer for himself," says the Policeman.

"Yes," says Zem, simply.

Behind his back, Zem curls his finger around a short, sharp knife lying on the bench top. He stands ready to strike at a moment's notice.

There is a long tense moment with the police looking

directly at Zem and Megan catches a glance of Zem holding the knife. The policeman flips his notebook closed and nods to his associate.

"Can you leave us a card?" asks Al.

"I'm sorry?" says the Policeman.

"In case we hear anything," says Al.

"If you hear anything, just contact your local police station."

The police leave and there is a collective sigh of relief and Zem uncurls his hand from the knife. Toddy sees them out of the apartment.

When the sound of the door closing is heard, Megan turns on Zem, "What the fuck do you think you are doing?"

"What?"

"You were going to knife two policemen for asking questions?"

"What were they doing here?" asks Zem, defensively.

"Who cares? They are police."

"They were armed in my house."

"That's because they are police!" shouts Megan.

"Why were they here?"

Al says, "They found a bag of our chop-chop at Danio's house."

"Well, how did they find us here?" demands Zem.

"Records, Zem, records!" shouts Megan. She stomps out to the balcony, leaving him looking bewildered. She stands with her back to the rail looking in at him. Her arms are crossed, and her face is red and curled up.

"Whoa," says Toddy, taken aback. "Hell hath no fury,"

"What does that mean?" asks Zem.

"Like a woman's scorn," says Al.

"*Ahhh*, yes," says Zem.

Dinner around the table is tense that night. Zem watches his Earth friends eating, feeling as though a distance has grown between them. Finally Al then Toddy then Megan wander off to their respective rooms. At last, Zem is alone with his thoughts.

One pressing though is that his so-called Earth friends are jeopardizing his mission. Now that the police have linked his house to the killings, his mission might already be dead. If Zem is questioned and found to have be without an Earth identity, he could be incarcerated as an illegal alien. Imagine that! It is for this reason that he must get a win with the bikers.

The small hours give way to the pale blue morning sky and Zem realizes that he has spent the entire night with gritted teeth thinking through the situation. Eventually, he hears the first noises of his housemates waking and he makes as though there were nothing wrong in his world.

He is pleased to notice that spirits are high again and the normal routine unfolds; Megan, Toddy and Al leave the house for the university, and Zem stays behind to study.

This morning, though, just sits on the balcony watching the boats in the marina, conscious of the seconds slipping past. He has mapped out a dozen alternative plans to working with the bikers should they not bear the fruit he needs.

Eventually, Zem hears the noise of motorcycles. He listens intently as they park down the road from the apartment block, in the place where they dropped him off the night before. He walks downstairs via the fire stairs and onto the street. Stovepipe is there with four others.

"Yo! Suit," says Stovepipe, directly. "We are back here in

two-hours. We are taking you to Melbourne."

"Melbourne?"

"It's a three-day ride. Keep your luggage small."

Zem watches as Stovepipe and his four biker mates rev up and depart.

He returns to the apartment, retrieves his bag, and takes it into the lounge room. The bag opens in his hands, and he retrieves the remote control on crystal meth.

Last Day

That evening, when Megan and Al and Toddy arrive home from university, they find that Zem has gone. Not only Zem, but also the Virid and his bag. They search the apartment looking for clues to his disappearance and Al finds it. The DVD lights are flashing suggesting that the power has been off in the apartment.

"He's been talking to the old girl again," says Megan.

The only other sign of Zem's passing is a pile of gold nuggets on the big glass table on the balcony. Toddy counts the nuggets.

"What do you reckon these are worth?" he asks, glumly.

"Oh, shut up!" shouts Megan.

She storms into the lounge room and flops down on the sofa. Al sits next to her, his arm around her shoulder and just looks distraught. Toddy walks in slowly, his head low. He sits on the floor with his back against the wall and for a long time no one speaks, they just stare sadly at the floor. A tear finds its way onto Megan's cheek.

Meanwhile, on the outskirts of town, pulled up on the roadside, Stovepipe and two of his men wait with their bikes. Zem remains on the pillion seat, patiently waiting as the seconds tick past.

Another five bikes approach, pull off the highway and park up. Tarp steps off one of the bikes and takes an approving look at the man on the back of the Harley Davidson wearing a fine suit and clutching a port that iridesces like the colours of a freshly caught fish.

Tarp slaps Zem on the shoulder and laughs. Zem just smiles, patiently.

Then Tarp notices the ten-litre plastic drum containing dark green liquid lashed to the pillion seat on Stovepipe's bike.

"What the hell is that?" he asks.

"It's a snack," says Zem. "Can we go now?"

"You sure are a cheeky little bandicoot," says Tarp. He Gives a signal and the bikers mount their machines and rev up.

"Ride well brothers," says Tarp, slapping Zem on the shoulder. The bikers drive off, taking Zemitheree Bedenifictu to Melbourne to get an official Earth identity.

Six Years Later

Tom Wayward's Den

Inside a plush den in the basement of a Louisiana mansion, a man sits in a large, leather lounge chair. He is obese with a bulbous second chin and white hair. Tom Wayward, the oilman, Chairman of Deepwater Petroleum, takes a sip of bourbon from a crystal tumbler and places the glass on the table next him. He reaches to the floor to retrieve a leather case.

In front of him, the television plays a current affairs show. In a studio interview is a white-haired man, Professor Jimmy Lovelace. Lovelace is tired, not because of his age, but because he is forced to explain complex and important issues in a format designed for entertainment.

Wayward glances occasionally towards the TV, not really listening. He is more interested in the contents of the case that he draws onto his lap.

The journalist says, "In your new book you say that eight billion humans have force Earth's natural systems beyond their Planetary Boundaries and will soon fail. What does that mean, fail?"

Wayward unzips the leather case and gently retrieves from inside a long metal object. Dull silver in colour, it is a Remington pump-action shotgun. He raises the weapon and squints along its length, panning it slowly around the room. Through the gun sights, he observes a collection of pelican heads mounted on the wall: hunting trophies from the Louisiana wetlands.

He shifts the gun to another part of the wall where five equally sized picture frames form a row. The first frame contains a photo of the massive oil rig, the Deepwater

Horizon, loaded on the back of a semi-submersible ship, en-route to the Macondo Prospect oil well in the Gulf of Mexico.

The next picture shows the same rig engulfed in flames and surrounded by emergency ships spraying huge plumes of sea water on the rig. This was the day that the rig exploded killing 11 men and commencing the largest accidental oil spill in history.

Wayward shifts the gun to the next picture which shows the Deepwater Horizon literally in deep water. After the fire, the rig sunk, one and a half kilometers to the bottom of the Gulf of Mexico.

The fourth picture shows the rig on the day she was raised from the seabed; a vast muddy and mangled contraption. Wayward lingers on this image, playing over in his mind the details of his pet project, the resurrection of the Deepwater Horizon.

He pans his gun across to the final picture frame. This one is empty. The project is not yet complete.

Wayward lowers the shotgun and retrieves a rag from the gun case and begins to polish the barrel of the gun sensuously. He looks up at the TV and hears Professor Lovelace speak with an anxious voice.

"The ocean is becoming acidified by carbon pollution. When the plankton die, our global ecosystem will lose the capacity to regulate its internal chemistry. And humans cannot survive without a good atmosphere."

"Have we passed a point of no return?" asks the journalist.

In the doorway of Wayward's den, his wife appears; she looks like him: large, stern, incomplete. "Are you coming to bed?" she asks.

Wayward turns his head just enough to make out her form in the periphery of his vision. "Just watching the news," he replies. Wayward's wife hovers in her place for a few seconds, lowers her head, then moves away.

Wayward turns a little more to confirm that she has gone. He resumes polishing the gun slowly, methodically.

Jimmy Lovelace tries to summarize his response to the journalist's question, "The biological system of Earth, the biosphere, is highly complex. There are many tipping points."

This answer is not good enough for the journalist. He is looking for something shocking, something newsworthy. "Well, have we gone past one?" he repeats.

Lovelace stutters, "One? It's not... Nature is not a bucket of water that you can pour out half and half remains. It behaves in the manner of a super-organism. Like a single living being. I couldn't chop you in half and expect you to be half the journalist you are now. You'd be dead."

The journalist turns this comment into a comedic interlude, "We'll leave that idea right there, if that's okay." He grins at the camera for effect.

Lovelace continues, desperately, "The scale and complexity of the risks faced by this planet has overwhelmed the capacity of any institution, any foreseeable group of institutions, to act in time. This is why we need all institutions to co-operate. In order for humans to survive on Earth, this planet needs an immediate..." Loveland places the palm of his hand against his face as though he is taking ill.

The journalist gives a second for Loveland to complete his sentence before prompting him, "An immediate?"

"I don't know," says Lovelace, wearily, angrily. "Humans are incapable of fixing the mess we have made. We need an intervention."

The journalist asks, "An 'intervention'... like?

"We need something we don't presently have," Lovelace snaps. He is done with the interview. He unclips his microphone.

Wayward watches this final exchange with mild interest. He gives the shotgun a final wipe with the rag then examines the weapon lovingly. He squints along the shiny barrel and aims it at the exhausted, frustrated scientist on the TV. He gently squeezes the trigger and enunciates a single word, "Bang!"

Townsville Airport

In the Townsville airport departure lounge, a short Irishman stands amid the crowd looking around impatiently, searching for something. He has a bag slung over his shoulder that carries an important document. He sees the coffee lounge and observes the red-haired female barista. She is mid-thirties, with an oval face and brown eyes. She carries a little more weight than she did in her younger years, but she is curvaceous because of it.

Erin, the Irishman, holds back for a few minutes until he has a clear run at the woman in the cafe without having to share her with the customers. When the coast is clear, he marches towards her. As he approaches, he sees her name badge and becomes confident that he has found the right person.

"Is it Megan?" he asks, directly.

"Hi," she replies.

"My name is Erin. I--"

He is cut off when she bellows across the coffee shop, "Flat white and a latte!" She turns her attention back to the Irishman. "What can I get you?"

"My name is Erin. Can I speak with you?"

"I'm a bit busy now, darling."

"It is very important," Erin says, impatiently.

"Well, so is caffeine. We've got this Brisbane flight, you see. What do you want to talk about?"

"I have a job offer."

"A job offer?" says Megan, laughing. "How cool is that? Do you run a coffee shop?"

Megan's female workmate takes her by the shoulders and

says to Erin, "We don't want to lose her."

"Don't worry Jo, I'll take you with me," Megan jokes.

"Take five, Megs, I'll cope."

Megan lets go of the coffee machine and steps out from behind the counter. She directs Erin to a table, and they sit.

"So tell me about this café," she says. "What's it called?"

"There is no coffee shop, Megan. I represent Mr. Anton Vorlov, from Vorlov Industries."

"Industries?" says Megan. "It's not a cleaning job, is it?"

"Mr. Vorlov requires a personal assistant."

"Cleaning his house?"

Erin stumbles, "*Err...* The role is supporting Mr. Vorlov in his daily duties."

Megan screws up her face, "What, is he sick or something?"

"He's very healthy, Megan, just very busy," Erin snaps.

"I get like that, sometimes," she says. "Too busy to clean up."

"You misunderstand, Megan."

"Well, what's the hourly rate, then?"

"It doesn't really have an hourly rate. There is an executive salary package which includes generous relocation expenses."

"Relocation? No way. I'm not going to the mines again. I did two shifts out at Gunpowder near Mount Isa. There were cane toads everywhere."

"It's..." Erin puts his face in his hands, sighing wearily.

"Are you okay?" asks Megan, concerned.

"It was a long flight from Dubai."

"Dubai? Is that where the job is?"

Erin retrieves from his bag a leather-bound folder. He slides it across the tabletop. He says, "It's all in here, Megan.

I need your answer before I leave."

"When are you leaving?"

"Right about now."

Erin looks anxiously at her, "There really is so much riding on this. It's not possible to explain."

Megan cocks her head and looks at Erin from a different angle, curious, "What flight did you come in on? What airline."

"Vorlov airlines, I guess."

"He's has got his own airline?"

"A couple of corporate jets and a million helicopters," Erin says, cryptically. He grabs hold of Megan's hands and squeezes them. She is surprised to see him close his eyes and mutter to himself.

"Are you praying?" she asks, concerned.

"No. I am willing you to read the document and say yes."

"Do you want me to look at it now?"

"Yes. Yes. Yes," says Erin, exasperated.

"Okay. Alright. Settle petal." Megan opens the folder and retrieves the paperwork inside. It bears a distinctive logo and the words: Between Destiny, a Division of Volrov Industries.

"Between Destiny?" asks Megan.

"Yes," says Erin, suddenly excited to be having the conversation. "Between is the philanthropic arm of Vorlov Industries. This document here is the salary package." Erin pulls one of the sheets of paper free and wiggles it in front of Megan's face.

Megan reviews the document, and her mouth falls open, "Is this a joke?"

"No. It's 'dinki-di'. Is that the right word?"

"This isn't one of those 'Gotcha' shows, or Candid... you

know?" Megan looks around the café expecting to see a camera crew but there is none. "I can't imagine what I would do that is worth so much money. Are you sure you have the right Megan?"

"Mr. Vorlov specifically requested you for this role," says Erin, disingenuously. He chews the inside of his cheek and looks at the floor wondering whether that he would ever regret having told that lie.

"He asked for me?"

"Well, sort of."

"When did I meet him?" asks Megan.

Erin goes into a tizz. He starts talking rapidly, winding up like he was going to explode, "Megan, don't ask me that. I am just the poor chappie who was instructed to leave his duties and fly across the planet to offer a barista a job worth quarter of a million dollars a year. I am not capable of understanding the quantum interconnections or the who did what to whom--"

"Okay, okay, okay," says Megan, waving her hands to settle the Irishman before he busts a blood vessel.

"I am sorry about that," says Erin, suddenly self-conscious.

"Well, that's okay. So what do you do there?"

"I run the schedulers," says Erin. "I set Mr. Vorlov's schedule. That's why I have to be back, you understand?" He leans forward hoping to entice her, "Ask me a question."

Megan shifts her body so that her head is close to his and she whispers, "Are you sure that I am the right Megan?"

Erin thinks it through, then asks a series of targeted questions, "Are you a barista?"

"Yes."

"Are you or were you a university student?"

"Yes, and yes."

"Do you live in Townsville?"

"*Durr.* Yeah," says Megan, emphatically.

"Are you – I don't know how to ask this properly – about thirty something?"

"No comment," she says, sternly.

"Okay. Final question," Erin says, looking at her name badge. "Is your name Megan?"

"It is."

"In that case," says Erin, "the chances of you being the wrong Megan are very small. Very, very small. In fact, I am prepared to wager a pint of Guinness – no, make that fourteen pints of Guinness – that you are indeed, the right Megan."

Megan glances back to the documents in the pouch and the salary package information. Then she sits back and observes Erin from a new angle. She sees the expensive knit of his clothing and his fresh haircut. And his tiredness.

"Just come and take a look at what we are doing, Megan. It really is mind-blowing."

Megan sits back in her seat and says, "You look exhausted."

"I am," says Erin, honestly, "We all are. All the bloody time. In fact, constant exhaustion is the only downside of working with Between Destinies."

Megan Arrives

Two Weeks Later.

Megan is seated in the front passenger seat of a sleek executive helicopter flying low across the waters of the Persian Gulf. Up ahead, approaching fast, is an archipelago, a cluster of hundreds of small, sandy islands. Most of them are vacant, just sand pads baking in the sun, but a few have elaborate structures built on one of them.

The chopper circles one of the outer islands and Megan hears the pilot's voice through her headphones, "This is Between Island. Your new home."

The chopper circles the island and Megan sees an extensive building complex with landscaped grounds. Solar panels cover the roofs, and wind turbines twirl in the sea breeze. From the air, Between Island looks like a resort or a campus, self-contained and complete.

Megan sees other helicopters buzzing around the island. There is a long jetty with five helipads, two on each side and one on the end. There are so many choppers in the air that it looks like a military operation is underway.

"It's busy today," says the chopper pilot. "That means Anton is home."

Megan's helicopter descends towards the landing platform at the end of the jetty. A tall Caucasian man walks towards the helicopter as it touches down.

"You must be important," says the pilot to Megan.

"Really?"

"That's Ollie, Mr. Vorlov's right-hand man."

Ollie walks briskly towards the chopper, crouches, and approaches. He pulls open the helicopter door. Ollie is angular, clunky fellow with warm eyes. He looks tired. "I am desperately hoping you're Megan?"

"That's me," says Megan.

"I'd say 'thank god' but I am not convinced that we need one to explain the world around us. I'm Ollie. Come on. Someone will get your bags."

Ollie helps Megan from the helicopter and hustles her down the jetty, walking and talking rapidly.

"Its crazy in there," he says. "One minute it's about carbon and next it's gorillas. Welcome to Between Island, by the way."

Megan can't keep with the pace, and her shoe comes off. "Hold up," she says, hopping back along the jetty to retrieve it.

Ollie watches as she adjusts her shoe. He takes her by the arm at the first opportunity. He says, hurriedly, "Megan, it's been like this for three months. Once upon a time we had a routine, but since we've been hitting on the oil guys it just madness." Ollie switches to an imitated voice, "Someone, somewhere, is awake." He goes back to his normal voice, "That someone ought to give him a damned sleeping pill."

Ollie pulls Megan to a halt next to one of the helipads as a slick, black Eurocopter Dauphin alights. The Dauphin is a space-age looking craft. The sound of its engine and blades thrashing the air sends a terrifying rumble through Megan's belly.

"You know who that was?" Ollie shouts over the noise of the chopper, "That was the C.F.O. of Deepwater Petroleum. Big jigsaw piece, that one."

"How many helicopters are on this island," asks Megan, watching a white Jet-Ranger, sporting the Between Destiny logo, touchdown. Two women and a man, dressed in suits, step out of the chopper and Megan watches as they walk briskly along the jetty, talking excitedly.

"There's five chopper pads and two jetties."

"It's so busy," says Megan, awed by the motion and pace.

"Busy?" Ollie seems to ponder, her statement. "That's an interesting word. Would you remind me to look into the sleeping pills?"

"He must work a lot of hours."

Ollie takes Megan's arm and continues along the jetty at a brisk pace. "His workload isn't human, Megan," says Ollie. "And now he has a personal assistant. *Ha!*"

They march off the jetty, onto a pathway that runs through the landscaped gardens. Ahead is the entrance to an elaborate building. Above the door are the words: *Between Destiny*.

"What does Between Destiny actually mean?" Megan asks.

"What we do here is create the opportunity for the humans to choose the future. We are helping to shift from the inevitable bad destiny to the chosen good destiny. Does that make sense?"

"Not really," says Megan.

Ollie pushes open the door saying, "I will rephrase and revert."

Inside the building, the hive of activity disappears, it is cool and calm. Glass prisms in the ceiling cast rainbow patterns. The floor is thickly carpeted, and there are lush pot plants lining the walls. A dozen or so people talk in small groups or check their mobile devices.

Ollie ushers Megan through another door to a sloping walkway that bisects a large chamber that is filled with hundreds of people. This room is the destination of all the people who fly to the island on helicopters.

Ollie pulls Megan to a halt at the top of the aisle. The room is dark except for a platform at the bottom of the walkway which is targeted by stage lights. One one side is a large screen that shows a jumble of constantly changing numbers. On the other side are video monitors with people paying close attention to the conversation that is under way between a man who stands in the center of the stage and another man whose face looms large on one of the video monitors.

The man on the monitor is Brenton Prest, the Chief Executive of Deepwater Petroleum. He is in conversation with the man on the stage, Mr. Anton Vorlov.

Vorlov is tall, strong, immaculately dressed in an Italian suit with python leather shoes. His demeanour suggests that he is most definitely in command of everyone and everything in the organization.

"How did you go with the C.F.O.?" asks Brenton Prest from the video monitor.

"He flew out a few minutes ago," says Anton. "I think he liked our proposal."

"Well, that's good news, then."

"I look forward to signing Deepwater Petroleum to the program."

"Not so fast, Anton" says Prest through the monitor. "We have internal politics to sort through. We have to sign off from Tom Wayward."

"Is that going to be a problem?"

"Old Tom has some pretty old ideas."

"What can we do this end?" Anton asks.

"A site visit to your algae oil farm for our board would help to answer some questions."

"Would Wayward come?" asks Anton.

"I can ask."

"We'll set it up, then," says Anton.

"Okay, let's do that," says the Chief Executive of the oil company. Then without ceremony, the conversation ends and the monitor showing Prest's face goes blank. The screen shows the Between Destiny logo, rotating slowly against a black background.

Anton Vorlov turns to the people in the auditorium and claps his hands together in congratulations. "Let's give it up for the good oilman," he says. There is a murmur of appreciation from the people in the crowd and light applause.

Ollie leads Megan down the aisle, towards the stage and as gets closer, she has a clearer view of Anton Vorlov.

She gasps out loud. "No way! It's Zem!"

The Auditorium

Ollie leads Megan to a table on the edge of the stage. "We'll just hang here for a minute," he says, quietly. As the discussion with the oil man has finished, there is a rotation of people going on. Some people are leaving the auditorium while others take their place. Above her, on the stage, the man they call Anton Vorlov is reviewing documents with one of his staff. The monitors above his head flicker and new faces appear.

Megan looks at Ollie, confused. "Anton Vorlov? Where's he from?"

"He's from Ukraine, officially. Off the record, he is… *Ummm…* Not from round here," says Ollie, cryptically.

"Thanks, Ollie, that's helpful."

"I don't know how much I am allowed to disclose."

A woman's face appears on the big monitor. She is grinning and her appearance seems to excite commotion from the people in the auditorium. The room is almost full now and there is an air of excitement. Something important is about to start.

Megan observes the activity taking place around the stage. She sees Erin, the Irishman who recruited her in Townsville airport. He has a headset on and consults a blue folder in which there are reams of paper.

All the commotion suddenly becomes formal when Erin addresses Zem, saying, "Mr. Vorlov on the big monitor is Candice Bergmann representing the Primate Project in the Democratic Republic of Congo. You will recall, Mr. Vorlov, that this project has been presented three times before. We think we you will buy this time. Okay, thanks Candice."

On the monitor, Candice looks down at Zem and says, "Thank you Erin. And hello to you Mr. Vorlov."

"Hello Candice. What do you have for us today?" says Zem.

"Mr Vorlov, we have addressed the concerns from the previous discussions and now offer the following. For sixty million dollars per annum over five years, we can police the eastern forests of the Congo and reverse the decline of the Silverback Gorillas and that of the Central African Bonobos. That's the pretty little chimpanzees. Biosec is in agreement."

From the crowd, a woman jumps up and shouts her support, perhaps a little bit too enthusiastically. The woman works with Biosec, the 'biological section' of Between Destiny.

"Thanks, Mary," says Candice, grinning. "This project makes people go a bit ape," she says, humorously.

"That's good, I like that," says Zem. "Write that one down, Ollie." Anton turns and scans the auditorium. "Where is the Swede when you need him?"

"Over here," shouts Ollie, waving. Anton turns to face Ollie and, by default, Megan too. She is suddenly struck with a terrifying chill that paralyses her. She does not want Zem to see her there. Fortunately, he looks right through her.

The danger passes and she feels adrenalin going cold in her veins. The murmur of laughter from the people in the crowd dies down and the dialogue about the primate project resumes.

Megan feels out of her depth and confused. She watches, stunned as the dialogue continues.

Candice Bergmann says, "The humanities section, Humansec, love the project, Anton, it provides jobs for hundreds of families, that's tourism services, security, parks management and so on."

"And Commsec?" asks Zem. Commsec is the commercial section of Between Destiny. Candice looks towards one of the other monitors where the Commsec representative is telepresent.

The man from Commsec says, "It's a big win for a small outlay, Anton. We think we can get an ongoing return from tourism revenue after four or five years. We run it as a non-profit that repays the principal over a decade. But the PR value for Between Destiny for protecting the gorillas… They are human ancestors, Anton, its huge."

"Okay," says Zem, "And Polisec?" Polisec represents the internal politics of Between Destiny and allows for the prioritization of projects.

A young woman from Polisec is in the audience, in the front row. She says, "No one opposes this project, Anton."

Zem says, "Four out of four. Good work. Spread the repayments over a decade, no interest required. This one is worth spending money on."

The auditorium goes quiet for a few moments while Zem confers with one of the people on the stage next to him. Then he turns to the man from Commsec and says, "Okay. Ape project. Buy!"

There is a noise from the people in the crowd, an excited chatter that grows louder as the transaction winds up.

Erin says, "Thank you Candice."

Candice says, "Thank you Erin. Thank you, Mr. Vorlov." Before she departs the monitor, she gives the double thumbs up to the crowd. "We saved the gorillas!"

Megan watches, fascinated as the people in the auditorium

erupt in cheers and excited chatter. Zem observes the behavior of the people in the auditorium and allows it to proceed for a while before he moves onto the next project.

"Erin," he says, and Erin consults his blue folder and directs one of his staff to mount the stage.

On the monitor now is a round face man in his mid-fifties. He has that highly pruned look peculiar to Americans. Zem, motions for Erin to proceed.

"Mr. Vorlov on the main monitor is Mr. Alex Vernon the Mayor of the City of Orlando, Florida, USA. Mr. Vernon has a proposal to apply ceiling insulation to all of the city's homes."

"I like ceiling insulation," says Zem.

"Mr. Vernon's project offers carbon reduction for U.S. three dollars fifty a ton. Total expenditure is three hundred twenty million over three years, but we get half of that back from the sale of the carbon credits. Biosec is not involved. Commsec is good to go, but Polisec has a concern."

Julia, the project manager from Polisec is on one of the monitors. She says, "Thank you Erin. Thank you, Mr. Vorlov. Our concern is simply the large sum of money allocated to a U.S. project compared to the sums that we have historically been funding to equivalent projects in Asia and Africa."

"We have already addressed this?" says Zem.

Ollie interrupts, "Anton, we changed the policy a little while ago. The Orlando project is the last initiative under the old policy."

"That makes sense," says Zem. "Polisec, you okay with this now?"

"Good to go. Thanks, Ollie."

"Okay, Erin, I am tempted," says Zem. "I do like ceiling insulation, but have we learnt from that debacle in Australia?"

Erin sends one of his staff onto the stage and presents a document to Zem. They review the document together.

Megan is taken aback by it all. She looks at Ollie for an explanation.

"What is happening here?" she asks.

"This is the Auditorium," says Ollie. "It's like a stock market floor. People come here to sell projects and Anton does the buying."

"Buying," says Megan, remembering Zem's stash of gold nuggets. "With what?"

"He's got twenty trillion dollars. See up there." Ollie motions for Megan to look at the large, illuminated board covered in numbers. The numbers show dollars flowing in and out of Between Destiny, hectares of reforested land, the CO_2 concentration of the atmosphere, and the acidity of the ocean. The numbers are in a constant flux.

"How did he get twenty billion dollars?" asks Megan, stunned by it all.

"That's trillion dollars, Megan. Trillion with a 't'. He's selling off his ruthenium alloy stocks. High temperature superconductors that he got from the seabed."

"I don't know what that means," says Megan.

"It means that your boss is a trillionaire and this auditorium is his supermarket."

Megan is taken nonplussed, "So what does he buy?"

"Right now, he's buying ceiling insulation in Florida."

"What for?" asks Megan.

"Carbon reduction and energy efficiency. And just before

he bought security for African gorillas. That's biodiversity conservation."

"These are environmental projects," says Megan.

"Yeah," says Ollie. "Plus, plus, plus. You remember that black chopper that took off when we were on the jetty and the oilman on the monitor a minute ago. That's the big project. Anton's trying to broker a joint venture with a consortium of oil firms headed by Deepwater Petroleum."

"How is that an environmental project?"

"It's not petroleum oil. Its algae oil that we grow in plastic tubes in the desert. It's green crude oil. Literally and metaphorically."

"Algae?" says Megan. She is reminded of the day she, Al, Toddy and Zem sat around the table on the balcony of the apartment and investigated the contents of his space bag. How did the conversation go that day. *Help me figure out what my mission is.*

She gasps and says aloud, "This is Zem's mission!?"

"Who?" asks Ollie.

"You call him Anton," Megan says. "This is his mission. He is doing environmental projects."

"Much more than that," says Ollie. "Your boss is bankrolling the restructure of the global economy to make it sustainable."

Megan looks up at Zem. He is talking with Erin about the ceiling insulation report. Around his head are dozens of computer monitors some showing the Between Destiny logo, others with people waiting on the outcome of the conversation.

"So that's his mission," she says again.

Ollie nudges Megan's arm and says, "Do you remember

Erin? I sent him to find you. He manages the four schedulers. They run shifts feeding projects to Anton. They help create the impression that he is human."

Megan does not know what to make of his statement. She looks around, bewildered, and sees Erin moving off the stage and Anton addressing the American man from Orlando on the video monitor.

"Thank you, Mr. Vernon. You will get your money shortly."

"Alright, you're up next," says Ollie. He ushers Megan towards the stage and addresses Erin, "Here she is."

"Oh wow," says Erin. "You arrived just in time." He takes Megan's arm and moves her towards the steps leading up to the stage.

Megan feels as though she is being herded. She struggles against Erin's grip and stops in her tracks.

Erin is a few paces ahead of her when he addresses Zem, "Mr. Vorlov, this is Ms. Megan from Townsville representing…" he turns to see Megan standing a few paces behind him with a red look on her face. "Well, Ms. Megan represents all of us, I guess."

"Thank you, Erin," says Zem. He turns his attention to Megan.

Megan Meets Anton Vorlov

Zem doesn't recognize Megan at first. His head is so full of primate conservation, ceiling insulation, oil industry transformation and a thousand other projects that he fails to connect the dots. He just stands there, looking down at Megan, trying to put it all together.

Her face is familiar and the name, too. He thinks back to a conversation a few weeks before when he was being hammered by Ollie about taking an Earth companion.

Zem had protested hard but under great duress had eventually said that he had one friend he would tolerate as a companion and that she was a university student who lived in a town called Townsville.

Megan from Townsville, Zem now thinks. Is that her? Six years on or is it seven? She was young then. A charming and enchanting Earth female. Now he sees a woman standing in front of him and she doesn't look happy. Zem is reminded of when she tossed the gold nugget on the table and berated him for offering to buy her friendship. She's wearing the same accusing look now.

Megan. Megan. Megan from the bush shack in the forest. Megan who put bandages on his wounds and cooked him the egg that he promptly spewed up. Megan who showed him how to use a mouse.

Megan is all of those things. However, in this instance, Megan is something completely out of Zem's paradigm and he is about to ask, "What is she doing here?" but he is struck speechless by the sight of her. He remembers that she tended his wounds on his first day on Earth. What is the earth word for someone like Megan? Associate? Helper? Friend? And where the hell does this fit into the program? What were the schedulers thinking?

Zem is rendered catatonic, staring at Megan. He feels stunned by the physiological sensation that comes from observing this woman. His heart rate shoots up and the pace of his breathing increases. He is motionless, staring into Megan's eyes.

"Oh shit," says Erin. "He's parked on her."

"Parked?" asks Ollie.

Megan looks at Zem directly. He is tall and powerful, standing on the stage surrounded by technology, lights shining down and hundreds of people from all around the world waiting on him.

She is unable to control the emotional upwelling that mixes anger and affection and sadness and happiness all together. What comes out of her is pure bolshie. "Well hi, Zem," she says directly. "Nice to see you again."

Zem takes a step towards the edge of the stage and descends the four steps, his eyes lock on hers. Across the auditorium there is the sound of a communal gasp; this doesn't happen.

Erin starts laughing nervously; his schedule is out by a minute now. "Mr. Vorlov are you taking a break?" asks Erin, shocked and confused.

"I'll take five minutes," says Zem, robotically.

"Five minutes, Zem," says Megan, angrily. "Is that it?" She turns on her heels and strides up the walkway not noticing a hundred pairs of eyes watching her.

Zem is surprised by her departure, and he follows her. Ollie is stunned to see Zem off the stage and he follows him up the aisle. Erin, his schedule shot to pieces, storms out of the auditorium after Ollie.

"Anton's taking a break?" says someone in the front row. A murmur of disbelief ripples through the auditorium.

Megan Overwhelmed

Zem catches up with Megan in the lobby. He directs her towards a door leading to a landscaped courtyard.

Megan shakes him free and protests, "Get off me Mr. sodding Vorlov," she growls. "What the hell is going on here?

"It's very busy," says Zem, lost for words.

Ollie appears like the ever-present minder, "Excuse me to interrupt. But Mr. Vorlov is in serious need of human intervention."

"Human intervention?" asks Megan, incredulously.

"I don't know how much I can disclose," says Ollie.

"You can tell her everything," says Zem.

"Okay," says Ollie, relieved, "It's not well known, thanks to our schedulers, but Mr. Vorlov doesn't actually sleep. You've heard of working 24 hours a day, well here he is. Years on end."

"Thanks, Ollie," says Zem.

Ollie continues, desperate to get it all out, "We can't take him anywhere without risking the authorities questioning which planet he's from, if you follow."

"No, I don't," says Megan, disturbed.

"You can go now, Ollie," says Zem.

Zem tries to takes Megan's arm gently but she pulls away waving her hands in the air.

She says, theatrically, "Overwhelmed! Will someone tell me what's going on?"

Zem looks at his watch, then ushers Megan through the door into the courtyard. It is beautifully manicured with lush vegetation. He moves a few paces to the shade of a tree with dark green, oval shaped leaves and bright white flowers.

Zem stands with his face to the flowers breathing in the rich aroma of frangipani. He breathes in deeply, slowly through his nostrils. "There is too much carbon in your atmosphere," he says.

"Hi, Zem," says Megan, with a challenging tone.

"Zem," he says, contemplatively, as though he had not heard the name in a long time.

"Hi, Megan," he says, but the intonation is not right. He is distracted, disconnected. Megan remembers the intimacy and familiarity of their time together in Townsville. Zem has been present in her mind every single day since he left. Now she feels as though Zem thinks of her as a one-night stand; that he can recall some fleeting details of the encounter but there is no emotion in it.

"Is that it?" she snaps.

Zem is lost. He makes to say something appropriate but just stumbles out with, "*Ummm.*"

"How about this, Zem," Megan says quickly, "Try saying: Hi Megan, how are Toddy and your brother, Al? Let me tell you a really compelling reason for walking out on you without saying good-bye."

Zem is nonplussed by Megan's reaction. He follows the words but the emotion pouring from her is foreign to him. He blinks repeatedly, totally unsure what to do.

"How are Toddy and Al," he asks, blankly.

"Well I don't see Toddy anymore and my brother, Al, tells me that if he ever met you again, he wouldn't speak to you."

Erin appears in the courtyard. He has an obsequious and direct manner that never fails to get Zem's attention. "I'm sorry Ms. Megan. Mr. Vorlov, we have the Prime Minister of

Sweden and his Energy Minister in forty-six seconds."

Zem is caught between Megan and Erin and for a second doesn't know which way to turn. He glances at Erin.

Erin says, "Oil industry restructure. Third discussion. The P.M. and the Energy Minister."

Zem sees Ollie inside the lobby and breathes a sigh of relief. He motions for Ollie to come.

"I have to go," he tells Megan and allows Erin to take him out of the garden.

He meets Ollie as he is entering the courtyard. "Ollie, help me out. I am really in the deep end."

Zem walks inside the building with Erin leaving Ollie to console Megan. He observes her standing under the frangipani tree looking stunned and angry.

"Megan," he says, hopefully. "I want to show you something."

Zem's Pad

Ollie walks Megan through the campus and swipes her into a private section where the interior is rich and dark. This is private quarters for Zem, Ollie, Erin, and a handful of other people in the inner circle.

Ollie ushers Megan into a room which she immediately recognizes as a version of Zem's bedroom in the penthouse in Townsville. It is stacked with bound technical documents and multiple computer monitors displaying news broadcasts and stock market trend lines and the like.

There is artwork on the walls, exquisite Art Deco paintings. Ollie observes Megan looking at the paintings.

"The paintings were my idea to try and humanize him," he says. "He likes the Art Deco, particularly the valiant looking people."

"What does that mean, to humanize him?" asks Megan.

"Soften him a bit, I guess."

"And that's what I am here for? To soften him?" Megan looks at Ollie, directly.

Ollie mulls it over for a second and decides that the truth is the best policy, "Yes. Again, my idea. I mop up after him and though that if he had someone, he could connect with on a level outside of work, then—"

"A friend?" asks Megan, disingenuously.

"Yes, like a friend."

"Well, this wouldn't be the first time he has offered to buy my friendship. And this is absolutely the bloody last!" Megan stamps her foot on the ground taking Ollie by surprise.

"It was my idea, not his. I badgered him to tell me the name of someone with whom he had connected outside of work. Eventually, in one of those rare moments you get with him, he said to me: Ollie, there is an amazing human, her name is Megan. I sent Erin to figure it out."

"So he didn't know I was coming?" asks Megan.

"Rationally, he knew, but I don't think it really connected emotionally, if you know what I mean. He's not a very emotional type."

Megan looks at the floor, confused. Ollie reaches out and touches her arm gently.

"A funny story," he says. "When Anton and I first met, he asked me if I was married. I told him that I was recently divorced. You know what he said?"

Megan shakes her head and raises a smile, remembering the *faux pas* of Zem from the old days.

"He said, that's good. And I said are you kidding me? How could that possibly be good, she was my childhood sweetheart, and I am still grieving, you heartless shit. He said, well its good because you will be able to concentrate on your work."

"That sounds like Zem," says Megan, grinning.

"And now he is saving the planet for us, if we can keep up."

"How are you going with that?" Megan asks.

"Well, he doesn't ever sleep. We have four teams each doing six-hour shifts and even they are exhausted because of his pace and because weekends and holidays don't fit into the regime. Our staff attrition is systemically debilitating but he can't see it."

"He stopped sleeping when he started drinking the Virid," says Megan. "Does he still do that?"

"The green goo?" says Ollie. "See that door?" Ollie points

across the room. He walks over and opens the door and Zem's room is suddenly flooded with sunlight.

Megan shades her eyes from the glare then steps into the Virid Room. Daylight floods through a skylight and the walls are all shiny white tiles. In the center is a large glass contraption the size of a brewer's vat. It has pipes leading into smaller vessels and it is filled with a dark green liquid.

Megan observes the Virid brewing device with awe, recognizing it from the fish tank on the balcony in the Townsville penthouse.

Ollie watches her from the doorway as she studies the device. "What do you know about Anton's heritage," he asks, intrigued.

"What do you know about it?" asks Megan, defensively. She observes air bubbles make their way from the bottom of the glass chamber through the dark liquid.

"Well, he's Ukrainian."

Megan laughs, "Are you serious?"

"He has a Ukrainian passport."

"He might have bought that, Ollie."

"Once he told me that he wasn't actually a human. I didn't want to know about that, so I just bought into the Ukraine story."

"Probably a good idea," says Megan.

"He looks human, but he is definitely a bit strange what with never eating or sleeping and working all the time. Where do you reckon he is from?"

"Well, he's not from Kiev."

"So my boss is a spaceman? How cool?" says Ollie, flatly.

"It's pretty cool," says Megan. She raises a smile realising that Ollie knows nothing about Zem's early days. Maybe she not powerless, after all.

"How did you meet him?" asks Ollie.

"Does anyone else know the spaceman story?" Megan replies.

"He's pretty tight with Erin," Ollie replies.

"How did you meet him?" she asks.

"I met Anton at a metals conference in Helsinki," says Ollie, cheerily. Anton said that I reminded him of his own people. I guess I was looking for a compliment and I said, 'Oh really, how so?' and he says, they are very boring and straight."

Megan giggles out loud, "Yep, that's Zem."

"Anyway, he recruited me to help him trade the ruthenium."

"The ruthenium? What is that?"

"It is a rare mineral. Very valuable."

"What's it for?" Megan asks.

"Power-lines."

"Power-lines? Like electricity cables?"

"That's right. Power-lines that don't heat up and waste energy. They call them high-temperature superconductors. Anyway, Anton knew of a huge deposit on the seafloor in the middle of the Pacific. Literally, in the middle of the ocean. I was so seasick."

"You went there with him,"

"Yeah. We were on that ship for months. We found the metal. Retrieved it. Sold it. And that's what we are using to bankroll the restructure of the global economy."

Megan completes her investigation of the Virid brewing device. She steps back into the office and Ollie closes the door.

She is more comfortable in Zem's space now and she observes the working desk, surrounded by computer monitors. Ollie picks up a small metal object from the.

"Here we go," he says. "This is ruthenium." He hands the piece of metal to Megan and she looks at in her hand. Instantly, she is reminded of the day that Zem emptied his bag on the balcony table. This was one of the objects inside. Back when he didn't know who he was or what he was good for. How long ago was that? Six years, seven years? She places the ruthenium on the table and notices another of the items from the bag, the little vial containing the Virid powder. Without Ollie noticing, she takes this and slips it into her pocket.

Suddenly, Megan feels tears well in her eyes and she just wants to be back home curled up in her bed under the covers.

"So how did you meet Anton?" asks Ollie.

Megan can't reply, she feels exhausted and sad. "Can you just show me to my room, please Ollie," she asks, weakly.

Ollie observes Megan's change of demeanour, and he doesn't know what to say. He leads her to the corridor.

They pull up next to a door where Megan's bags are stacked. Ollie fumbles in his pocket for an electronic key, swipes the door and opens it for Megan to step inside.

"Thanks, Ollie," she says seeing her bags inside.

Ollie hands her the keys and begins to say, "Nice apartment, huh?" Megan closes the door on him.

Inside the apartment, Megan rests her back against the door and looks around. Being in her own personal space isn't really helping that much as she is intimidated by the opulence, the marble, the heavy drapes, the artworks.

She moves to the bay windows and observes that she has her own private beach. It is all so beautiful and perfect, it's overwhelming.

Megan walks into the bedroom and sees the king-size bed with its matching linen. She flops down on the bed and curls up in a ball. She blinks and sniffs as tears well in her eyes. Through the lace curtains she sees the little beach outside the window and the sea beyond.

Who's Responsible?

Between two and five a.m. in the Between Destiny HQ there is a self-imposed blackout in communications to the outside world which helps to preserve the appearance that Zem actually sleeps. During the blackout, Zem continues to work on emails which are embargoed until morning.

Erin and Ollie hang around in Zem's office, winding down from the long day before they wander off to their rooms to sleep for a while.

Tonight, Ollie has a new enrolling mission, and he arrives at Zem's desk with a tray covered with a tea towel.

"I invite you to join me in a week of innovation," he announces and then ceremoniously removes the towel to reveal a China tea pot and a single cup.

"Decline," says Erin, automatically.

"How is that innovative?" asks Zem glancing up momentarily and then looking back to the email he is chopping out of the computer.

"I am pouring your Virid," says Ollie. He lifts the teapot and angles it over the cup. Zem glances up with a concerned look, as though Ollie was interfering with a cultural ceremony. However, the Virid is so viscous that it doesn't pour, and Ollie stands there looking like a still from an Alice in Wonderland movie.

"Does it do anything else?" asks Erin, smugly.

"What are you doing, Ollie?" Zem asks.

"I'm diversifying your ritual," says Ollie, now shaking the tea pot to force at least one drop of Virid to fall from the spout.

"You've done that, alright," Erin snips.

"Why?" asks Zem, perplexed.

"Well..." says Ollie, lost for words. He pats the tea pot on its bottom but still no green liquid falls from the spout. "I am trying to make you more human," he says.

Erin chimes in again, saying, "With all due respect Swede - which ain't that much by the way - but you are hardly a suitable candidate for that role."

"What is that supposed to mean?" asks Ollie, defensively, taking off the lid of the teapot and peering inside.

"You brush your teeth twice in a row," says Erin, matter-of-factly.

"Does he?" asks Zem, looking up briefly from the computer.

"I have never seen anything like it," says Erin. "He even puts the cap back on the toothpaste before he starts round two."

"That's bizarre," says Zem, without look up.

"You see, Ollie, even the spaceman who never needs to brush his teeth because he drinks green goo every day thinks that you are weird."

Ollie plonks the teapot onto the tray, takes the tray by the handles and moves it away.

"Okay, send," says Zem, striking a finger against the keyboard then rubbing his hands together as though getting ready for business, "Erin and... Where has Ollie gone?"

"He's sulking."

"What does that word mean?"

"It doesn't matter. *Ahhh*, here he is."

"Okay, how did Megan come to be here?"

Zem looks directly at his two men, but they avoid his eyes.

"Someone be first."

"Well we all did," says Ollie.

"What does that actually mean?"

Ollie continues, "It means there was a general consensus that we would be better able to meet our operational targets if you spent some time one-on-one with a human."

"A real human, that is," says Erin.

"And Erin, you went and found her, right?"

Erin clears his throat. He is in the spotlight now. He says, "You muttered something about red hair, beautiful, Townsville, student, coffee shops. Nothing about cranky, mad bitch. But anyway, I took it from there."

"Well, you brought her here, so I suggest that you ensure that she is properly looked after," says Zem.

Erin and Ollie look at each other blankly, forlornly.

"Now, I am going to put the final touches on this J.V. proposal to Deepwater Petroleum and you guys, probably need to get some sleep.

"Yeah, four hours," says Erin. "Thanks. Anton."

Chat with Ollie

The next morning, Megan takes a call from Ollie. She is in a combative mood and talks quickly, "How am I Ollie? I'm angry. What? Well, maybe you expected it. It would have been really nice if someone had told me that I would be working for *Zemitheree Beden-ifictu*. Who? Okay Ollie, you can call him Mr. Vorlov but I will call him just whatever the hell I please. Now, if Erin had told me who my boss would be I would have told him to shove the job up his hairy Irish ass. Excuse the French. What? Okay. Come round for a chat? What? Okay, I will calm down."

By the time Ollie arrives, Megan has discovered that her apartment comes complete with a San Remo Verona coffee machine and all the supplies she needs. Ollie is treated to the full experience of a professional barrista: the racket of the bean grinder, the hissing noise of the milk frother, and the deep aroma of Arabica coffee.

Ollie watches Megan at work on the machine choosing his words. "Erin said that you were a barista."

"It was actually a really good shift at the airport," she says. "It paid the bills while I was studying."

"What were you studying?"

"I'm like a professional student, Ollie. I've been at uni for years. I probably would never have left if not for this job." She looks at Ollie directly. "This is a job, isn't it?"

"It is a job, Megan, you will see. What were you studying?"

"I am onto my masters now. It is sort of a hybrid between psychology and environmental science with a bit of anthropology and eco-tourism thrown in. For the field trips, mainly."

Megan hands Ollie a cup of coffee and takes a seat at the glass table with him. "I am sorry if I was a cow yesterday," she says.

Ollie chuckles, "That's okay, I think you gave Anton a bit of a shock, though."

"Serves him bloody right," she says, without remorse. "So what's the plan for my first day on the job?"

Ollie retrieves a document and refers to it. It is one of the schedule documents that shows day after day blocked out with commitments, twenty-four-seven.

"We have a break in Anton's schedule at eleven forty this morning. He's in the Greenhouse."

"The Greenhouse?" asks Megan.

"That's what we call the office on the mainland. The Greenhouse. The Techno-garden. The Anthill."

"Right," says Megan, not really sure what that means.

"So if you are up for it, meet me at the chopper jetty at eleven and we'll go over."

Megan mulls it over, feeling as though it were an offer she could just as easily accept as reject. "A break in his schedule, huh? How long's that for?"

Ollie refers to his notes and clears his throat. He looks around nervously, not sure how to break the news.

"Ten minutes," he says, eventually. "Is that okay?"

Empowered and Anxious

Later that morning, Megan walks with Ollie to the helicopter jetty. Unlike the day before, when she arrived, there is no swarm of choppers flying in and out and droves of professionally dressed people chatting excitedly. In comparison, the island looks empty.

"Where are all the people?" she asks.

"The action follows Anton around," he says.

Megan looks across the sea to observe a sleek executive helicopter powering towards them. It is a white Sikorski with a pale green stripe on the lower fuselage and the distinctive Between Destiny logo. The chopper thunders around the island and descends towards the landing pad. Megan recognizes this as the chopper she came in on and she entices a nod from the pilot when their eyes briefly meet.

The sensation of being near the helicopter as it lands is overwhelming. The high pitch howl of its turbine engines synergizes with the thrum of the propeller blades thrashing the air. Its resonance is felt as much as heard and all around there is a storm of warm air with an unmistakable aroma of fresh popcorn. The size of the craft and the way that its great bulk descends from the sky is at once dangerous, and yet the knowledge that the craft is there for her creates a sense of bravery and empowerment.

"What's the popcorn smell?" Megan shouts to Ollie.

"She's running on algae-biofuel."

"How come whenever I ask you a question, I don't understand the answer?" Megan shouts back.

Ollie shrugs. He crouches and approaches the helicopter. He pulls open the door and beckons Megan to enter the craft. He follows her onto the white leather seats and draws the door closed.

The inside of the helicopter is air-conditioned with a TV monitor and a bar fridge. Megan pulls the seatbelt around her waist, clicks it closed and pulls it tight. For a second, she feels lightheaded, as though she has, in a day, become an expert and getting into helicopters; something she had never even considered doing before.

As the chopper alights, Megan feels the gravity shift in her stomach and hears the high pitch of the engine resonating through her body. She looks down at the island campus and identifies the roof section that makes up her apartment and her little beach.

Seeing the island from above brings with it a sense of empowerment. Her new job allows her to command the actions of great machines. It permits her to twist her nefarious boss Anton nee Zemitheree around her finger to avenge her sadness and that of her brother, Al, and her ex-boyfriend, Toddy.

The chopper flies at speed towards the skyscrapers of Dubai and the sun-baked archipelago flashes past underneath. Megan's emotions change and now she feels a knot form in her stomach. It is a mixture of anger, sadness and most of all anxiety knowing that she will soon be in Zem's presence again.

The Greenhouse

The Between Destiny office tower, the Greenhouse, rises eighty floors above a landscaped island in the desert behind the city of Dubai. Seen through the front windows of the helicopter, it initially appears as a pale blue shimmer on the horizon. However, as the chopper comes closer, finer detail emerges. Megan is no scholar of architecture, but she can see that great minds have designed this building.

The lower third of the building has an outer covering of lush vegetation, looking like a cliff face adjacent to a waterfall. The verdant skin is surrounded by birds flitting in and out. It appears that the Greenhouse has been constructed as much for wildlife as for humans. Indeed, it appears that the building is itself a part of the wildlife.

There are multiple chopper landing pads that extend out from the upper levels of the building. These are recognizable as such because of the swarm of helicopters landing and taking off. What did Ollie say? Where goes Zem, so go the choppers.

Beneath each of the landing pads, hanging like a giant strand of DNA, are vertical axis wind turbines spinning freely in the breeze. These great structures are twenty meters in height and whisk the higher-level winds into a froth of electrons that surge into the building.

The chopper swoops a wide loop around the Greenhouse. Ollie taps Megan's arm to gain her attention, but she is so engrossed in the visual spectacle of the building that she does not notice.

Midway up the building is a floor from which grows a great forest. Vegetation hangs over the edge in long green tendrils.

Through this foliage crashes a torrent of water, a waterfall that descends five floors and is arrested by a protuberance that directs the flow back into the building.

Megan is intrigued. From where comes this great flow of water, she wonders? As the chopper circles, she searches up and down to resolve the mystery.

Had Megan read the brochure about the Greenhouse she would have known that the white panels that extend from the exterior of the building from floors 35 to 45 were fog harvesters that extracted freshwater from the moist air that rolls in from the Persian Gulf. With no added electricity or mechanical assistance, the panels strip water vapor from the air and turn it into a thousand trickles. The trickles combine into a dozen torrents that form into a single gushing river that runs in a helix channel down and around the perimeter of the building before cascading into the rainforest.

On a lower floor there is an indoor farm where people can be seen tending vegetables in racks. Above this floor, extending out from the building are sheets of mirrors that reflect sunlight into the building from where it is distributed to the vegetables.

On another floor, around the perimeter, is a running track with people jogging a thousand feet in the air. And at the very top of the building, a spire that contains what looks like scruffy bird's nests but is, in fact, a much-used artificial substrate upon which native birds of prey have built their nests and raise their chicks with a grand view of Dubai, and not a penny to pay in rent.

Megan is dumbfounded and quite rightly so. There is no architecture on Earth like this building. She shakes her head in wonderment and eventually she notices Ollie tapping her arm.

"This is the first," he says. "Self-sufficient in everything. Even falcon eggs. That was a joke. Anyway, we have orders for eighty of them around the world, each designed specific to their climate and eco-zone."

Megan doesn't follow all of this but understands one thing. The building is further testimony to the vast capacity of *Zemitheree Beden-ifictu* and the scale of both the opportunity and the risk associated with her position with him. She finds herself in awe of the man just from looking at his architecture. She does not know how to behave appropriately around him and has only her instincts to guide her. This is cause for concern because Megan is unsure whether her instincts are up to the job. The knot in her stomach returns, tighter now.

The chopper descends towards a landing pad and the Greenhouse a.k.a. the Anthill looms closer and closer until the fantastic structure is the only thing visible through her window.

"Why do they call it the Anthill?" she asks Ollie as the chopper touches down on the pad.

"White ants," says Ollie. "The air conditioning system was designed by termites."

Another meaningless answer, she thinks. Then she realizes that somehow the air conditioning system probably was designed by termites. This insight only serves to stun Megan into a sense of having fallen down a rabbit hole into Wonderland. She feels giddy, like Alice on opium.

Ollie slides open the door of the chopper and the warm breeze from the Gulf sweeps into the cabin. It brings with it the distinctive aroma of Dubai: a subtle blend of petrol fumes and dust mixed with Arabian oils and tea rose perfume.

Ollie offers his long, bony hand and she accepts, allowing him to guide her from the chopper into the Greenhouse. As she steps inside she hears the glass door slide closed behind her with a contented whisper. Even the doors like being in this building, she thinks.

For Megan, the inside of the Greenhouse is on a different experiential scale to flying around the outside within the confines of an air-conditioned helicopter. Stepping inside is like coming home.

Tinfoil Hat

The first thing that Megan notices is a great commotion and the sound of children laughing and shouting, and adults trying to keep them in order. The noise reaches a crescendo like a riot of fun.

"What's that?" asks Megan.

"Some rock star that Anton has invited," says Ollie.

"A rock star?"

Then the man in question shows up. He is tall and handsome, with a shock of bushy hair and face paint that makes him look like a cross between a clown and band member of KISS.

"That's Ying Stravinsky," says Megan, amazed.

"You know him?" asks Ollie.

"Everyone knows him. He super famous. Why is he here?"

"Marketing," says Ollie. "Connecting Between Destiny with popular people, whatever."

Megan beams a smile, stands on tippy-toes and waves, calling out, "Hi, Ying!" but Ying is too distracted by the kids to hear her.

"How cool is that?" says Megan, excitedly.

"Come on," says Ollie. "This way."

Ollie leads Megan into a corridor where training rooms occupy a whole floor of the greenhouse. Each room is full with attendees from all corners of the world; different colours, different dress styles. Megan stops and observes one of the training sessions in progress.

Ollie tells her, "This floor is dedicated to the Between Destiny education program."

"Wow," says Megan.

"We call it the Curriculum for the Living Planet."

Megan moves further along the corridor, intrigued. The training rooms are circular with a small podium near the far wall. Thirty students face inwards and the presenter talks facing the door into which Megan is looking. In this manner, anyone who walks past can get the benefit of the lesson. Megan is intrigued by the efficiency and openness of the education facilities. She is able to listen to each of the lessons and observe the presentations, typically with rich multimedia and colourful props. She stops by one of the rooms and overhears the presenter.

"Today, there are eight billion humans on Earth, that's eight thousand million. And every year there are seventy million more. And all these good people need to be fed, clothed, housed, and entertained."

Megan moves to the next session and listens in, "On Earth there are nine biophysical systems with threshold boundaries that need to be protected in order to ensure a safe space for humanity. Most of these so-called Planetary Boundaries have been crossed."

Megan moves onto the next class and here a young male presenter sees her and draws the attention of the class to her. "Now here is a lady who know how to dress."

"Who me?" asks Megan, embarrassed.

"Yes. Perhaps you could give us some practical clothing advice for a trip to the Moon," he says.

Megan is unsure how to answer and she searches around for some context to the question. On the door there is a sign announcing a class titled the Greenhouse Effect.

"*Ummm*. A spacesuit," she offers.

"And you are not wearing a spacesuit right now, are you?"

asks the man, rhetorically.

"*Ummm*, no," Megan replies, grinning.

"Well, consider this," says the presenter. "On the sunny side of the Moon the temperature can get up to 107 degrees Celsius, that's enough to boil water. However, when the sun goes down, the temperature plunges to minus 153 degrees. So in the day you'd need to wear, I don't know... Shiny metal suit with a tin foil hat." There is a murmur of laughter from the people in the class.

"And lots of sunscreen," says Megan.

"Lots of sunscreen, yes. And at night, you be wearing a big puffy, thermal underwear, gloves."

"Five pairs of socks," Megan says.

"Five pairs of socks. And you can imagine the mad dash to change clothes when the sun goes down," says the trainer.

"So what is the lesson?" asks Megan, confused.

"Well, it's not like that on Earth because some of the gases in the air around us absorb heat and they smooth out the temperatures. We call these greenhouse gases. Now if didn't have these greenhouse gases, we would need to change our clothes very quickly at dusk."

"Right," says Megan.

"In fact, our problem is the opposite. Right now, we have too much greenhouse gas in the atmosphere."

"Right," says Megan.

The presenter acknowledges her and says, "Thanks for your input, Miss..?"

"Megan."

"Thank you, Miss Megan," he says and elicits a little round of applause from his study group.

That was fun, Megan thinks. She looks around for Ollie

who is waiting on her at the door to the lobby area. Megan walks towards him but stops instinctively when she sees a tall African woman speaking with a thick Cockney accent conducting one of the classes. She wears stylish glasses and hot pink fingernails.

She informs the class, "If our economies and societies operate within the constraints of the Earth Systems, then humans could conceivably live on Earth for a Galactic Year. And that's what Between Destiny seeks to achieve by restructuring the global economy."

Megan finds herself motionless, stuck in a trance. She thinks of all the sleek helicopters buzzing around with the smell of popcorn. She thinks of the auditorium where Zem buys environmental projects. And the amazing Greenhouse building that she now stands in. The world-famous rock stars bought in to connect the kids to the brand. And the sheer order by which all these elements interlock and function as one. And all this to win the biggest game in town; allowing the humans to enjoy their birth-right, a synergistic relationship with the biosphere, deep into the Long Future.

Megan feels giddy, stunned by the scale of the enterprise and its audacious, hyper-ambitious goal. It is too big for her, she thinks. It is too big for her to even play a small part in. She begins to fret, feeling alone and overwhelmed.

She looks up and sees Ollie motioning towards her. That annoying man who bought her into all this and who never gives a straight answer. Megan finds herself hypnotically walking towards him.

Solar Panels

Megan is led through the building towards a maze of conference rooms. It is busy here, a lot of people moving and talking. She looks around at the intense people locked into the mission, giving it their best. The bustle of busy executives suggests that Zem is close by.

Ollie checks his watch and tells Megan, "He should be out in four and a half minutes." Then he ushers her to step out of the traffic flow of people surging from one meeting to the next.

Megan stands by the ceiling-to-floor smart-glass window and looks out across the desert. In the distance, she can see the skyscrapers of Dubai and beyond them the Gulf. Out there somewhere is her apartment on Between Island but all she can see is a hazy smudge.

She is alerted to a quiet but distinct noise like that of a small brass bell being struck four times: *Ting. Ting. Ting. Tingggggg.*

This noise triggers an automatic reaction amongst the people on this floor and suddenly Megan's position by the window is shared with a dozen strangers pressed up against the glass and looking down towards the desert floor.

Ollie says, "Look, up there," and he points to the one of the vertical axis wind turbines. "See it's slowing. The wind has dropped. The solar panels will come out."

Five floors below there are long tubular structures extending horizontally from the building. Along their upper surface are faint lights that start to twinkle with the colours of a rainbow. The tubes open and from within a device that looks like a folding fan extends.

This concertinaed material is not for moving air but for harvesting the energy of photons from sunlight. The solar panels shimmer with pale blue crystal patterns as the fan opens, stretching out dozens of meters horizontally. When the fan is taught, fully open, the entire structure, rotates to better align the surfaces to the direction of the sunlight.

Megan is awestruck and fails to notice the jostling as the workers in the building feast their eyes on the spectacle.

Suddenly, the ambiance changes and Megan turns and looks up, straight into Zem's eyes. He is standing there, solid, like he was cast from the same material as the building itself, looking straight into her mind.

Megan gasps and sees all around him his entourage, dozens of executives with clipboards and folders, all anxious to get his attention. Erin is there, looking worn out. He has Zem's itinerary in the blue folder, weeks upon weeks of meetings structured twenty-four hours per day. No time in the schedule for a beer, a night off, a long weekend; too busy to piss, as they say.

"Hello, Megan," Zem says, calmly.

Megan goes to say 'Hi, Zem' but all that she can muster is a squeak noise, like a mouse confronted by an alley cat. Damn her instinct, she thinks.

"These solar panels are very efficient," he says casting a proud eye over the huge aquamarine fan extended below them. "But they kill worker productivity."

"Yeah, back to work you guys," snaps Erin and the people in the crowd by the window scatter in all directions.

One of the staff hands Erin a mobile phone and whispers in his ear. Erin absorbs the message then touches Zem gently on his arm and says, "Anton, in three and a quarter minutes, we have the meeting with the United Nations Environment Program, four floors down and..."

Zem continues to hold Megan's attention. She is completely entranced, and she can see him forming a smile. It doesn't appear in an instant. Instead, it germinates, probes delicate tendrils across his cheeks, as though to test whether it is safe. Megan is paralysed, fixed on the growing facial expression.

Erin says, "Anton, I have Brenton Prest on the phone." Brenton Prest. Chief Executive of Deepwater Petroleum.

Megan watches as Zem turns his head to Erin. She observes a robotic inevitability in his movements as he takes the phone. He places it to his ear and focuses his gaze over her head and a thousand yards beyond the floor-to-ceiling, smart-glass windows.

"Brenton," says the non-stop, planet-saving machine called Zem. With that one word, Megan knows that she has lost him again. Within a second, Zem's entourage have turned in perfect synchronization as he walks away with the phone pressed to his ear.

Megan observes a sea of backs receding. The hallway empties and she suddenly feels as though she is standing a thousand feet in the air above a desert, all on her own. Then she sees the one remaining human; a tall, lanky Swede who observes her with a new expression; something conciliatory. Without speaking, he seems to be saying, "Sorry for bringing you into this."

Busy Schedule

Megan returns to the island in Zem's helicopter with Ollie, but she does not speak to him. She watches the flat surface of the Gulf flash past, and it hypnotizes her, shutting down her thoughts.

Back on the island, she steps off the chopper and marches along the jetty, through the campus and into her room. It is not until she has slammed her apartment door behind her that she feels as though she can express herself. She bursts out laughing and wipes away a tear that has trickled out of one eye.

"Sod him," she says, exhausted for caring. She slumps down on the sofa and stares at the floor.

Back at the Greenhouse, Zem concludes the meeting with the United Nations Environment Program and moves straight to one with the World Bank. He pulls up outside the conference room where thirty people are arranging themselves around the table.

"You should schedule some time with Megan," he tells Erin.

"No way," snaps the Irishman. "Last night you said you didn't want to have anything to do with her."

"That's right, Erin. And I have changed my mind. Can you make it happen?"

"Well, how long do you want?"

"I don't know. What do you reckon?"

Erin checks the schedule. He flicks through page after page, muttering to himself.

"We have got an unallocated fifteen minutes in ten days."

"Is that all? Anything sooner?"

"Not unless we flip something."

"What's to be flipped."

"Well," says Erin, trying to nut it out. "If you wanted something soon, we could flip the Russian Snow Leopard project."

"No," says Zem. "Biosphere integrity have to take priority."

"Okay, we have the Vanuatu energy restructure, shifting from diesel to geothermal."

"No, energy projects are critical. Climate change, Erin, very important."

"*Hmmm.* Okay how about this one, you were going to put a billion into a public transport system for Karachi, India. You know how their bureaucracy is, they probably won't be ready."

"That was the light rail. I like light rail. Here's an idea. Do you think it would be possible to combine Megan with a meeting?"

Erin lowers the blue folder and looks at Zem with an expression of astonishment. He shakes his head. "Are you suggesting that you conduct business whilst simultaneously hanging out with an Earth chick?" asks Erin, stunned.

"Can we do that?"

"Ollie is right. You just don't get it."

"Well, what would Earth people do in this situation?" asks Zem, frustrated.

Erin pushes open the door into the board room and thirty people from the World Bank look their way. "Think about it later, Anton," he says. "Think about it later."

An Agreement

Later that night, Zem is in the Auditorium having conversations with people on the other side of the world, where the sun is still shining. A meeting is about to start when the woman on the monitor apologizes profusely.

"Mr. Anton, please be excusing us, the board is present, but the C.E.O. is stuck in traffic. He assures that he will be here in fifteen minutes."

Zem turns to Erin, "What are we doing with these guys."

"Rehabilitation of the Dominican Republic fisheries. A billion dollars over ten years," Erin tells him.

"*Hmmm*. Seafood. Important source of protein for millions of people," says Zem. "Okay, I'll be back in ten minutes."

"You'll what?"

Zem steps of the stage and walks up the aisle. Ollie, who is half asleep at his desk next to the stage, is suddenly wide-awake and watching his boss move rapidly up the aisle.

"What's happening."

"You brought her here, you figure it out," snaps Erin.

Ollie jumps to his feet, and scurries up the aisle, "Anton what are you doing?" he asks, anxiously.

"I am going to speak with Megan."

"Do you know what time it is?"

"It's daytime somewhere, Ollie."

"Yes, but it's one a.m. here."

Zem stops and asks, "What's the significance of that?"

"She'll be asleep."

"But she will wake up, right?"

"Of course."

"And then she will go back to sleep," says Zem.

"Yeah."

"So what's the issue?" Zem continues on his way. He swipes into the private quarters and reaches Megan's door. He raps firmly and checks his watch. He continues observing his watch, counting down the seconds when the door pulls open a little way and he sees Megan's face. She has a distinctive look; puffy with squinting eyes. Zem is taken aback.

Megan grunts a sigh, "It's you," she says. "Surprise, surprise." She opens the door and Zem steps inside.

"You too, Ollie," she says.

Zem asks Megan, "Are you comfortable here?"

Megan rests against the glass kitchen table, struggling to wake up. In this state she is very calm and clear-headed and cuts straight to the questions she most wants to ask.

"I don't understand, Zem. Why me? Why invite me here?"

"Ollie convinced me that I needed a human intervention. His words. I remembered you from..." Zem looks at his hands and feels a pang of something. What is that one called? Remorse? He suddenly wishes that he had explained his departure to his three friends. He mumbles something then says, "I remember you."

"We spent about three months together and then you just split without a word," Megan says. "We never even got to... You know."

"What?"

Megan turns to the Swede, "Ollie, could you get something from the beach for me."

"Sure. What?"

"I don't know, a stone fish, a blue ringed octopus. You choose mate." Megan walks towards the door that leads to

143

the beach, collecting Ollie by the arm on the way. She hustles the lanky Swede outside the building, then closes and locks the door behind him.

She moves back to the table, more awake now and feeling her emotions rising. "We were never lovers," she says, plainly.

"That's not why you are here."

Megan is surprised at the frankness of this statement.

"Right," she says, at once relieved and upset by this news. "Ollie makes these cryptic comments that you are an alien or something. We used to call you a spaceman because it was funny, and it seemed to fit but I don't actually know anything about you."

"I have a disc that will help explain things, it's a video presentation. I would like you to see it."

"Sure. I'll watch it. So is your name Zemitheree or Anton?"

"Anton is my Earth name."

"And Zemitheree?"

"That is my real name. My Parrathean name."

"Parrathean?"

"We are hominids, like humans, but we have been intelligent longer and we…" Zem stops, suddenly realizing he has never really tried to enunciate his alien heritage before. Except to Erin who bought in instantly, no details required; and to Ollie who refused to believe that he was anything than Ukrainian.

"So you are a person from another planet?"

"Yes," says Zem.

"Great," says Megan, folding her arms. "My boss is an alien. No wonder we don't get on. Should I ask which planet?"

"Parrathea."

"Where is it?"

"It's out there," Zem points to the ceiling.

Megan shakes her head and wipes her palms across her face. This is too much to deal with right now.

"What am I doing here, Zem?" she asks flatly.

"Megan. Please be patient, there is a lot going on right now. We're trying to joint venture our algae oil technology with a petro…" Zem stops talking as Megan abruptly adjusts her pose.

She shifts her hands to her hips and sets her jaw looking directly at him. Zem meets her eyes briefly and then he looks away.

Megan says, "Sit down, Zem. Have a coffee."

"I can't do that."

"You can't sit down, or you can't have a coffee?" she snaps.

Zem mumbles and Megan watches him with eyebrows raised.

"How about you just sit down, then," she points to a chair. "Sit down, Zem. I will only keep you for three minutes."

Zem check his watch: there is enough time for that. He sits and watches as Megan paces in a circle, forming her words.

"Zem, I want the planet saved as much as the next person, but let me be clear about something."

"Okay."

"When you are around me, don't talk business, okay?"

"Okay," says Zem, relieved.

"Do you want me here?"

"Yes."

"What for?"

Zem mumbles again. His eyes flick to various parts of the carpet, looking for an answer.

"To help you be more human?" asks Megan.

"Yes?" he says.

"Are you sure about that? Because when I get my teeth into something I go like a psycho vampire," Megan emphasizes this point by shaking her hands with her fingers held like claws.

"I don't know what that means," says Zem.

"Do you want me to help you be more human or not?"

"Yes. I do."

"That's a real yes? Your intuition says yes?"

Zem is suddenly aware of an opportunity. Being more human is a strategic move that will help him get what he needs from the other humans; maybe they won't quit and grumble so much. Plus, he can use the excuse of learning humanness to be closer to Megan and he would really like that; for every time he is her company, he feels physiological changes in his body that are exciting to him. He resolves to tell Erin to be more lenient with the schedule with respect to Megan-time. Maybe he can set a one-hour session per week. Zem finds himself nodding. The answer is intuitive, and he expresses it as such.

"Yes," he says, and his tone makes it sound as if he means it.

Zem observes Megan's demeanour change and instantly the tension departs the room. Her frown eases and she feels magnanimous. So she offers him what he most desperately wants.

"You can go and play with Ollie now."

Zem gets up from his seat and moves to the door. Before

he exits, he turns and glances at Megan and does something extraordinary. He smiles.

Between Billions

Days later, returning from a trip to London, Zem, Erin and Ollie step into the white Sikorski at Dubai International. Seated inside, they are in high spirits, discussing the trip.

Erin retrieves a notebook from his pocket and ceremoniously raises a pen preparing to write. "So, I am putting a tick next to 'billionaires' on the list of priority groups for the big climate talks," he says.

"How's the list looking now?" asks Ollie.

"Not so bad, Swede. We have done governments, artists, business leaders. And after our trip to London, I am ticking off the billionaires. *Tick.*"

"So what's the latest thinking on the climate talks," asks Zem.

"We are looking at around 70,000 delegates coming to Dubai to finalise the plan for the transition to clean energy."

"Who's taking the lead on that?"

"You and United Nations Secretary General."

"Okay, who's next on the list of priority groups?"

"The militaries."

"I don't understand why we have generals on the list," says Ollie. "What can we ask them to do?"

"Transition to algae biofuels," Zem says. "Just because they try to kill each other, they don't have to kill the planet in the process."

"Ecologically sustainable warfare," says Ollie. "I can't quite get my head around that."

"Ask them to go easy on the nukes, too," says Erin.

"Why don't they just not to go to war in the first place?" asks.

"Once we have swapped petroleum oil for algae, there won't be much to fight over anymore," Zem says.

"The Billionaires Club was inspired genius," says Erin.

"Between Billions," says Zem. "Did you like that?"

"I love it. Ten percent of the world's billionaires pledging ten percent of their net worth annually to the transition program."

"How much did we get from that?" asks Zem.

"About a hundred billion," says Ollie.

"What should we buy with that, lads?" asks Zem, rubbing his hands together as if he is preparing for a shopping spree.

"Biosec keep haranguing me about this program called Don't Snub Me that is worth about $5 million," Ollie says.

"Don't Snub Me?" asks Zem. "What's that for?"

"It's a program to stop the Australian coastal dolphins going extinct."

"Don't Snub Me," laughs Erin. "That's classic."

"I don't get it," says Zem.

"It's a dolphin joke, Anton," says Erin, dismissively.

"The genius of Between Billions," says Zem. "Is Phase Two."

"There's more?"

"Of course. Who would want to be a billionaire who is not in the Between Billions club?"

"Not me," says Erin.

"Leveraging off Phase One is Phase Two is when we get the 20% of the billionaires to commit 20% of their net worth. How much is that worth, Ollie?"

Ollie closes his eyes and performs a mental calculation, "Wait. That's… That's a squillion. Or two."

"You could save entire planet for that," says Zem.

Erin shakes his head and looks out of the chopper window. "Just to think, before I took this job--"

"Before I offered you the job," corrects Ollie.

"Yes, and thank you for reminding me the thousandth time," Erin snaps. "As I was saying, before I was offered this job I used to worry about my mortgage."

"Have you thought any more about scheduling me some time with Megan?" asks Zem.

"No I haven't, actually, Anton," says Erin, curtly. "I've been a bit preoccupied with little things like scheduling meetings with world leaders and funding biodiversity conservation projects across the planet."

"Is that it?" asks Zem, seeking more.

"Plus, I was thinking if I didn't mention it, you might just forget to ask."

"Well, that didn't work. Anything else?"

"I was thinking that if we ignore her, she might just go away."

"How does that sit with you, Ollie," Zem asks.

"What am I?" asks Ollie, abruptly. "Megan's mother?"

"Ollie made a joke," says Zem, laughing.

"Not a very bloody good one, though," scowls Erin.

Zem looks at his two men and concludes that he is out of step with them with respect to Megan and that he should just put her out of his mind. He looks out the window to see a fleet of helicopters heading towards Between Island. There are Jet Rangers, Long Rangers, Dolphins, and Squirrels. It is the entourage speeding in for another gathering in the Auditorium. What's next on the schedule he wonders. That's right, another chat with Brenton Prest.

Zem checks his watch and says, "Yeah, you are right.

Deepwater Petroleum will be telepresent in three minutes and forty seconds. Stick to core business."

Egg Sandwich

In the days that Zem has been feting billionaires, Megan has been taking it easy on her own. Initially, her spirits were high following the early morning discussion with Zem. She spent the first day enjoying her luxury apartment and laying in the sun on her own private beach.

On day two, a routine was established. Wearing a colourful bikini covered with a light, cotton sarong, orange thongs and garish sunglasses, her travels extend no further than moving back and forth between her deck chair and the kitchen where she mixes daiquiri cocktails, rich with fresh fruit and white rum.

On day three she called Ollie and got an international dial tone and a message bank. She left a message asking for an update, but no reply came. Later she sent him a terse text demanding a response.

Now, on the fourth day of the binge, she stares through bleary eyes at her mobile phone where she has discovered Ollie's reply to her text message. The words are indistinct, but she thinks she reads something about a change in the schedule.

"Oh no, a change in a schedule!" she says aloud, parodying Ollie's voice, "Ve are goin' to change the schedule. Noo! Noo! Ve can't change the schedule." She stops, realizing that she is talking to herself and observes the empty cocktail glass and the empty beach. Pissed in paradise; how many daiquiris is that today?

Her attention is broken by the sound of a fast-approaching machine. She nearly leaps out of her sarong when a huge, sixteen-seat Eurocopter flashes past between the palm trees with a booming noise like a drumroll. The is the first of a dozen choppers that announces Zem's return to the island.

The noise disorients her and she is rendered motionless as she watches the sky fill with executive helicopters zapping past. One minute she is on a peaceful tropical island and the next, the air is humming with ultrasound as the flying machines thunder past. She wants to run away, but she is too incapacitated to move and all she can do is sprawl on her deckchair watching the sleek choppers circle the island, one after another, preparing to land.

She can see Zem's entourage peering at her from their noisy sky chariots as they swoop towards the landing platforms. The noise of the machinery is ear-splitting, and it rises and falls as the aircraft flash past.

Megan suddenly feels self-aware. Here she is lying around getting smashed while Zem's team are hard at work transforming the global economy to make it sustainable.

Then Zem's white Sikorski, rumbles past sending shock waves rippling through her belly and forcing her into the apartment. She finds herself standing in the kitchen looking at the mess from days of binge drinking.

The holiday is over, she thinks. She lets out a growling noise, feeling as though she is being violated or punished for not having been gainfully employed. Time to get to work, then. So what was her job? She is the personal assistant to Anton Vorlov.

"That's a big mission he's on," she tells herself. "And he doesn't eat properly. So…"

Megan pulls open the fridge door and examines the contents. She rummages around for ingredients and sets about fixing the most fabulous egg and salad sandwich ever created. She fusses on this special project until the meal is perfect. Then she places it on a tray, sets a garnish with a frangipani flower from her little garden and steps into the hallway.

She walks purposely into the Auditorium with the sandwich held in front of her. She doesn't notice that the room is full and there is an excited buzz. Zem is standing in the middle of the stage in discussion with Brenton Prest, whose face looms large on the main monitor.

Brenton says, "We are just about to pitch the joint venture proposal to Wayward. We will be pressing pretty hard to overcome any arguments he raises."

Zem nods appreciatively and asks, "How much power does Wayward have?"

"He's the Chairman," says Prest. "And majority shareholder. He can appoint and sack directors. It's his company, Anton."

"Okay, well good luck," Zem waves to the monitor. Prest's face fades from the screen and Zem turns to his scheduler, but a very strange sight catches his attention.

Megan walks down the aisle wearing her bikini and sarong and her overt sunglasses. Her skin glows from three days sunbaking. White rum oozes from her pores like perfume. She looks - and smells - like she has just stepped off a photo-shoot for a Bacardi advert.

She approaches the edge of the stage and holds up the tray showing off the sandwich. It is stacked with boiled egg, lettuce, tomato slices, mozzarella cheese and a Middle Eastern chutney that smelled delicious when she opened the lid. She has cut the crusts off and sliced the sandwich diagonally.

"Mr. Vorlov," she says, directly. "I made you an egg sandwich."

Instantly, all eyes in the auditorium are directed towards Megan. In her colourful beach clothes, she stands out like a carnival in a desert.

Zem stares at Megan and his jaw falls open, amazed at the colour of her skin and her clothing. He is mesmerized by the pale line of flesh at the top of her breast that had been hidden from the sun beneath her bikini. The warmth of her body radiates towards him with an intense and sensual aroma. He feels as though a huge velvet spider has grasped him and draws him towards its jaws.

"Eat the sandwich, Zemitheree!" Megan instructs, firmly.

Zem is mesmerized and he follows the instruction. He lifts one piece of the sandwich from the plate, bites it in half and stands there like a condemned man chewing his last meal, staring into Megan's big, brown eyes.

"Bloody hell," says Erin looking around desperately, the blue schedule folder falling from his hands. He staggers back against a table, awestruck, fearing what comes next.

Zem swallows the first part of the sandwich and pauses, but he is instructed firmly by Megan. "Eat it all up," she demands. "There's a good boy."

Zem puts the remainder of the sandwich in his mouth and chews it. A little blob of chutney drips on his chin and he raises his finger to wipe it away. He swallows the remainder of the sandwich.

"Thank you, Megan," says Zem, his voice, strained. He looks anxiously at the second half of the sandwich and is relieved to see Megan lower the tray. She smiles broadly, turns on her heels and walks away, taking the rest of the sandwich with her.

Ollie descends the Auditorium aisle and passes Megan on the way. He observes the half sandwich and the state of the crowd. He looks at Erin who is standing, gob-smacked.

"What happened?" Ollie asks, but Erin is unable to reply.

One of the other schedulers says, "Vorlov's P.A. just offered him an egg sandwich."

"And?" asks Ollie.

"And he ate it."

"Oh, f**k."

On the stage, Zem is looking really sick. He is swaying, unable to concentrate. Ollie leaps up and catches him as he staggers forward, "Erin, help me!"

Erin and Ollie move Zem off the podium and half carry him up the aisle, out of the auditorium. They march him through the lobby, through the sliding doors into the corridor where Megan stands outside her room, pointing for them to carry Zem inside.

They drag him into the bathroom from where comes the sound of puking and retching. After a period filled with the noise of running water and spluttering, Zem comes out of the bathroom, his face red. He slumps in a lounge chair as Erin and Ollie flap about him like startled seagulls.

Megan pokes the toe of her orange flip-flops against his leg. "What's the matter Zemitheree?" she barks. "Don't you like my cooking?"

"What the hell, Megan? You can't feed him!" shouts Erin.

She turns on the Irishman and barks him down, "You bought me here you little paddy shit! You want me to turn him into a man, well here's the routine! The boy needs a good feed!"

"I think she's been drinking," says Ollie.

"Wake up, Swede," growls Erin. "Haven't you seen the kitchen? It looks like a frat-house. Megan! Mr. Vorlov is not human. He doesn't sleep. He doesn't eat, drink, shit. He doesn't even fuck, for all we know."

"He doesn't fuck? Is that right?" says Megan, seeing an angle.

She stands with her knuckles clenched, resting on her hips, looking like a mix between a beach bunny and an angry dominatrix, bearing down on the three helpless men.

"Zemitheree doesn't fuck. Huh?" she says again. She kneels down in front of Zem and pouts her lips, "Poor little Zemmy never had a shag."

Zem turns his face to Megan. Her aroma is intoxicating - literally. He says nothing, her colours and the radiant heat pouring from her stun him into silence. He looks at the curves of her body through the thin sarong and the sheen of her waxed legs. And he just grins.

Humans of Earth

Next morning, Megan wakes with a pounding headache and spends the morning in the apartment with the drapes closed. She sits in the dark thinking through the activities of the previous day. She is not upset by it, feeling somewhat empowered, really. She now knows that she can prize Zem away from his entourage if she wants.

Later she takes a call from Ollie who says that he wants to pay a visit. He enters the apartment cautiously and dithers like an indecisive stick insect.

"I am sorry if I shouted at you yesterday," he mumbles.

"You didn't, Erin did," says Megan.

"Well, I am sorry if Erin…"

"You don't have to be. I will take my awful revenge against Erin at a time of my own choosing," she says, ominously.

She watches Ollie stewing and says, "I'm just mucking with you, Ollie. I got a bit drunk and acted up and here we are."

"Yes," he says, cheering up a bit.

"Is there something you wanted, specifically?"

"Anton asked me to give you this," he says retrieving a memory stick from his pocket and handing it to Megan.

"What is it?" she asks.

"He calls it the disc, even though it is a memory stick. Anyway, you can plug it into the big TV over there. It is some sort of video presentation about his background."

"Have you seen it?"

"No. I don't indulge in the spaceman story."

"You'd rather he was just an oligarch from Ukraine," Megan, grins.

"It's easier that way."

Megan shows Ollie out of the door and then searches the TV for the slot where the stick enters. She spends a few minutes fiddling with the remote and eventually finds a channel with a blank screen with the word 'Play' and an arrow in the center. She sits on the couch with the remote and starts the video.

The video shows two elder males - Torreth and Verten - who are in a heated discussion. They wear the distinctive prosthetic adornments that Megan had seen the old woman wearing in Zem's video call. There is a third person there but because they are in the shadows, their face is not visible at first. The two men speak a foreign language, but there are English subtitles underneath.

Torreth: What is there to know about the hominids of Earth? What are they called? *Homo sapiens*?

Verten: They are on their way out.

Torreth: So soon?

Verten: The influence of their fossil fuel elites is causing the collapse of their biological systems.

Torreth: *Hmmm*. How bad is it?

Verten: Their oceans are contaminated with synthetic micro-plastics, and acidifying from carbon pollution. Their atmosphere is heating rapidly.

Torreth: Do the humans protect their iconic species?

Verten: *Pah*! As if. Their big cats are nearly extinct. The great whales, the same. Even their own evolutionary ancestors the apes and chimpanzees are critically endangered.

Torreth: What about boundaries of their biophysical system?

Verten: Most Planetary Boundaries are crossed. The nitrogen cycle is overwhelmed.

Torreth: Greenhouse gases?

Verten: Over 400 parts per million.

Torreth: That's a tipping point just there. Their green technology?

Verten: Their algae biofuels are clumsy. Their PV is okay, but only covers a small percentage of energy demand. Wind technology is good but made from non-renewable materials. Huge financial subsidies favour fossil fuels. The fossil fuel elites are stalling...

Torreth: Yes. Yes. I get it.

Verten: The biosphere will soon lose homeostasis.

Torreth: That would be the end of the complex life.

Verten: They need a takeover.

Torreth: There will be no support for risking our forces. Is there anything special about them, as a race?

Verten: They can be very religious.

Torreth: There's an angle. Maybe we make an appearance. Tell each of the religions that we are the God-Head. Stir them up, let them war, and drop their population numbers.

Verten: No. They have fission and fusion weapons. The radiation will retard the evolutionary development of their biosphere by tens of millions of years.

Torreth: How many nuclear weapons?

Verten: Thousands. Including megaton-scale, multi-warhead systems. There's enough for a mass-extinction event.

The third person at the table moves into the light, an elder female. Hearing her voice, Megan is jolted into full attention. It is the woman that Zem spoke with in the apartment in Townsville.

Music: Will you two stop arguing! We are not going to let the humans of Earth perish. There will be no nuclear wars, and we will not be invading the planet either. We'll see them through their Anthropocene Crisis and into the Verdant Age.

Verten: We are out of time, Music.

Torreth: Do you have a plan?

Music: We'll restructure their economy to make it nine-boundaries safe.

Torreth: That will cost trillions.

Verten: They spend that much on their wars. It's not like they don't have the money for it.

Music: Send an Agent with superconductors. We have millions of tons of ruthenium alloy sitting around, doing nothing. He can sell it. That will fund the transition.

Verten: A government will steal it.

Music: Teleport it to the seabed. Give him the coordinates. He will retrieve it, and that will fund is mission.

Torreth: And some green technology, maybe?

Music: The Agent should take fuel algae and solar crystals. Develop joint ventures with energy firms.

Verten: Do we have such an Agent?

Music: I know a Parrathean who can achieve this.

Torreth: And if the oilmen refuse?

Music: Use the Hammer.

Verten: The Oilman's Hammer?

Torreth: The Hammer? *Cough!* Really?

Music: I will authorize the Hammer.

Verten: You won't get it past Kelver. He hates humans.

Music: I have locked horns with Kelver in the past

and I will do it again. But I need your support?

Torreth: Okay, I'm in.

Music: Well that's decided then. I will set it up.

Verten: Tell the Agent to keep the Hammer close by.
Oilmen can get very precious about their hydrocarbons.

Chairman, Deepwater Petroleum

In Houston, Texas, the boardroom of Deepwater Petroleum is busy with an Extraordinary General Meeting to discuss the Between Destiny joint venture proposal. There are fourteen on the board, and the only one not yet present is Tom Wayward, the Chairman. Brenton Prest is there, seated next to C.F.O. Brenton observes the edginess in the other board members, but he himself is calm.

The sight of a large shadow moving rapidly along the frosted glass wall announces the Chairman's arrival, and the doors swing open. Tom Wayward storms into the boardroom. His face is red, and he has three shots of bourbon in him and freshly brushed teeth. He stands in the doorway looking at his board with contempt.

A secretary moves past him, cradling a pile of documents. "What's this?" Wayward barks.

"Minutes from the last meetings," she says, instantly cowed.

Wayward takes the documents and drops them in a trash bin, saying, "I only need one minute to sort this shit out."

Wayward moves to the head of the table and berates his Chief Executive, "What's this bullshit about a joint venture with Between Destiny?"

"Hi Tom," says Prest. He can smell the toothpaste on Wayward's breath and knows what to expect.

"I give you the keys to my truck, Brenton," Wayward snarls. "Don't crash it into Lake Shit."

Prest has a karate black belt and over six years dealing with Wayward. Despite the aggression, Prest says calmly and plainly, "This is a good proposal for the firm, Tom."

Tom Wayward leans on his knuckles and growls, "Don't forget that old Tom who birthed the company is an oilman."

"It's an oil project, Tom," says Prest. "Fifth generation algae oil that is set to blow gold."

"But old Tom is a *petroleum* oilman. Not a god-damn pond-scum oil-man!"

The director of public relations addresses Wayward, "Tom, we all appreciate the cultural sensibilities, but this is a win all round; economically, socially, environmentally."

Wayward fixes the PR man with a glare and then ominously moves around the table to stand behind his seat. After a few moments feeling Wayward's bulk emanating heat at him, the PR man steps away from the table and leaves the room.

Wayward watches him go and says: "That's one less bit of fruit on the sideboard. Social. Environmental? What is this, Save the Pelican Day?" Wayward looks at each one of his board members in turn. The only one who meets his eyes is Prest who observes him placidly. "So it's a good deal, is it Brenton?"

The C.F.O. says, "Mr. Wayward, the financial projections for the green crude are exceptional. Because this oil is grown, not pumped it—"

"I am not talking to you!" bellows Tom Wayward, and the C.F.O. shuts up immediately.

Wayward moves over to Prest and eyeballs him at close range. "It's a good deal is it, Brenton?"

Prest says, "Tom. Listen to me." He waits until Wayward gives an indication that he is prepared to hear him out. "The supply of our raw material, petroleum oil, is getting harder to extract. Furthermore, because of global climate policies –

whether you believe the science or not – our petroleum reserves are soon to become a stranded asset. Un-burnable carbon, Tom. The Between Destiny algae oil grows and grows and will never run out. Plus, it burns with no net carbon emissions, so we can continue to produce oil without exposing ourselves to litigious carbon policies. We write off the upstream assets, locate the algae farm on the petroleum lease sites, and continue to use our refinery and distribution infrastructure. We are in the oil business forever."

Prest has had Wayward's attention for about as long as he thinks he can hold it, so he closes, changing his intonation, "We should take the lead on this inevitable change in our industry, Tom. The J.V. with Between Destiny will... blow... gold.... all... over... this... firm."

Wayward leans close to Prest, and says quietly, "You are missing something, Brenton."

Prest sits back in his seat. He gently clasps his fingers together, "What is that, Tom?"

"I am a *petroleum*-oil-man, and this is a *petroleum*-oil-company. It's what I know. It's what I do. It's what like. It's that simple."

Wayward points his finger at his board members one by one, "If I hear of this project again, I will replace every one of you pond-scum mother-f**kers with real oil people! Even if I have to sue every one of you to get you out of my life."

Wayward's face is red and sweaty. He pans around to each of his board members and watches as they avert their eyes. Only Prest is watching him, silently, impassively.

"Now," says Wayward. "Because I want to go to heaven, I am prepared to meet this Anton Vorlov character. And the upcoming Houston Oilman Awards is the place to do it. Set it up, Brenton. Get him a seat on my table."

Prest observes that the entire board has fallen into submission. He shakes his head, ruefully.

"Now," says Wayward. "Anything else on the agenda?"

Job Interview

A few days after the incident with the egg sandwich, Megan calls for Ollie to visit her and when he arrives, she asks, "Ollie can you get me a meeting with Cassie, the Head of Human Resources?"

"I guess," he says, noncommittally.

"You guess?"

"I'm not sure that that is such a good idea."

"I need a job, Ollie, a real one. I can't spend my days as a Personal Assistant who doesn't get to assist. It's doing my head in."

"Don't you have any hobbies?" he asks.

"Ollie, I live in a luxury hotel room on a tropical island. What hobby would I have that doesn't involve abusing the minibar? I need a job."

"Well you could ask Cassie, I guess."

"That's what I just asked for."

"Okay, I'll set it up."

Megan watches Ollie staring at the floor, cursing his luck.

"Today?" she asks.

"Today?"

"Yeah. Like you have influence and authority. So..."

"Okay, okay. We'll go over."

Ollie wanders outside and makes a call on his mobile phone. When he returns, he says, unenthusiastically, "Come on, we'll go over now."

"Excellent," says Megan and she whisks into the bedroom to dress accordingly.

Forty minutes later, the helicopter touches down on the Greenhouse helipad. A secretary ushers Megan into Cassie's office. There is a large, hardwood desk behind which the head of Human Resources sits reviewing a document. She has her head down, as if a deliberate rebuff to Megan. Megan looks at the top of Cassie's head and glances out the window across the emptiness of the desert. She is reminded of the expression: as without, so within.

"Hi Cassie," says Megan, taking the seat in front of the desk.

The H.R. Manger looks up and repeats her own name, "Cassie?"

"Yes. Hi. I am Megan."

"Do I know you?"

"I am Megan."

"What I mean to say is: I don't know you," says Cassie, curtly.

"I am Megan?" Megan says again, unsure where the conversation is going.

"I ask this because I didn't hire you, Megan," Cassie grumbles, "Because if I had hired you, I would know all about you. I would know what you were good at. And what you were absolutely and pitifully hopeless at."

Cassie clasps her fingers together, interlocking them in such a manner that her gold rings form a single block of metal studded with gemstones. Her fingernails are varnished, and Megan becomes aware of the smell of Cassie's perfume. It clashes terribly with the jewellery: gold, diamonds and air freshener, something like that.

"Well, would you like to?" asks Megan, hopefully.

"Would I like to what, Megan?"

"Hire me."

"Hire you for what? Catering? I hear you make a mean

sandwich. Mean, being the operative word."

Megan pauses and looks at Cassie's jewelled hands for a beat, trying to find her way. She feels her heat rising but desperately wants a win.

Cassie continues with her abuse, "If I had wanted to hire you, don't you think I would have done so already?"

"I have an environmental science degree and I tutor," says Megan, hopefully. "Maybe I could be one of your trainers."

"Oh, you are interested in education, are you?" says Cassie with sudden enthusiasm.

"Yes, I am," says Megan, excitedly, thinking that the dam has broken.

"Well that's fantastic," says Cassie. "Because there is some knowledge that is sorely missing in this organization."

"That's great, what is it?"

"I do the hiring and firing for Between Destiny, not Ollie! And you will never have a proper job in this organization. And by the way, what is it you actually do here?"

"I don't know," says Megan, briskly. "Ask the old cow that runs H.R. Apparently she knows everything."

Megan gets up from the chair and turns to the door. She steps into the reception area when she hears Cassie's final retort following her out the door.

"You can tell Ollie that there are millions of unemployed people. He'll be in good company."

"Tell him yourself, you fat bitch," shouts Megan, then storms into the hallway. She sees Ollie ending a phone call and stomps towards him.

"That was quick," he says. "How did it go?"

"Oh, really well," says Megan, disingenuously, quickly shifting her demeanour. "Cassie asked if you would pop in to say hi, she wanted to thank you."

"Oh really," says Ollie, lightening up. "What for?"

"I am just the messenger, Ollie."

"No worries, then," says Ollie. He shines a cheesy grin and wanders into the H.R. department. As soon as he is through the door, Megan sweeps through the building back to the helipad and instructs the chopper pilot to take her back to Between Island.

Back in her apartment, she retrieves ingredients from the fridge and sets to work creating a cocktail big and complex enough to calm her down.

"Now this," she says, gritting her teeth. "This is a real hobby."

Party Invitation

After a forty-second exchange with Cassie, Ollie staggers out of the H.R. department and leans against a wall, recovering his composure. He has sweat trickling down his neck and a cramp in his stomach.

Eventually, he looks up to see Zem depart a meeting room and he wanders over to join the entourage. Zem sees him and dismisses the group.

"I am going back to the island," he tells Ollie. "What are you doing?"

"Yeah, whatever," says Ollie, distracted.

"Call the pilot. I'll be back in a minute."

Shortly, Zem and Ollie are seated in the helicopter with the turbine engine winding up. Zem lifts the armrest to reveal a refrigerated compartment containing a steel bottle. He removes the cap and takes a long swig of chilled Virid.

"There's an email just come in from Brenton Prest," says Ollie, looking at his smartphone.

"Did they like our proposal?" asks Zem.

"The board loves it but Wayward is not buying in."

"I thought he was a businessman," says Zem, perplexed. "They are going to end up with billions of dollars-worth of un-burnable oil. What's he thinking?"

"His daddy was a wildcatter," says Ollie, looking out the window as the chopper ascends and moves away from the Greenhouse.

"What does that mean?"

"He has a long family tradition in petroleum."

"Well, I don't get it."

"You don't understand humans, Anton. That's why we

171

insisted you have quality time with one," says Ollie, glumly repeating his mantra. He continues to scroll through the email.

"Megan. Yes," Zem says, thoughtfully.

"Here is an angle," says Ollie, "Wayward has invited you to the oilman awards in Huston."

"What is that?"

"To quote the email, a celebration of the successes and the characters of the petroleum oil industry."

"Why would I go there?"

"You could use your charm on Wayward. And take Megan with you," says Ollie, suddenly alert. "Yes, take Megan with you."

"Take her to the party?"

"You would be expected to have an escort," says Ollie, suddenly in love with his own idea.

"Do you think she'd go?" asks Zem, curious.

"She'd love it. She's still upset about the sandwich thing. And you haven't seen her since then."

"Do you think that Erin could squeeze it into the schedule?"

"I'll make sure of that," says Ollie.

"You really think it's worth going?"

"Let's put it this way," says Ollie. "What's preventing Between Destiny shifting the global economy to clean energy?"

"The oil industry is not at the table," says Zem.

"That's right. And what's holding that up?"

"Tom Wayward from Deepwater Petroleum"

"So, you charm him. He comes around. And it's all good."

"Okay," says Zem. "Buy. Would you pass the information

to Megan?"

Zem sees Ollie's the sour expression. "What's the matter?"

"Megan is not my favorite human right now."

"Have you been arguing with my assistant?" Zem chuckles.

"Anyway, it is customary to invite her to the party, yourself."

"Where is she?"

"Probably in her room, sulking," says Ollie.

"What does that word actually mean?" asks Zem.

"It means that she is thinking of you."

"Oh, okay. And how long will the invitation take?"

"About three minutes."

"We'll need to change the schedule."

"Do it as soon as we land," says Ollie. "We can cut into the meeting with the International Monetary Fund."

"Cut in? You mean turn up late for the I.M.F?"

"Just by a few minutes."

"But I am never late for meetings," says Zem, astonished.

"A fact that has not gone unnoticed in capitals around the world," says Ollie, grumpily. He turns away and looks out the helicopter window.

Zem sees the back of Ollie's head and wonders what the change of mood indicates. The chopper circles Between Island.

Down below is the little beach in front of Megan's apartment. And there, seated on the deckchair is Megan. She looks like a butterfly with her bikini, sarong, orange thongs and outrageous sunglasses. Zem sees the shape of her body through the soft silk fabric, and he observes her look his way and adjust her glasses. Their eyes meet for the briefest moment. What he doesn't see is the cocktail shaker in the ice bucket next to her.

Zem looks back to Ollie, wanting to say something nice about Megan, but Ollie is still acting grumpy. He is suddenly anxious to be out of the helicopter and talking to Megan. He wonders whether Ollie has enough clout with Erin to get the I.M.F. meeting delayed, maybe cancelled altogether.

An Awesome Proposal

Erin and a group of six professionals are waiting on the perimeter as the white Sikorski touches down. The chopper door slides open and Zem steps out. He crouches and moves quickly beyond the reach of the blades, then straightens up to full height.

He strides along the jetty with the entourage surrounding him like ducklings. Erin, who has the shortest legs of all, struggles to keep up. "What's next," he asks, looking ahead, without breaking his stride.

Erin starts talking as rapidly as his legs are moving, "Anton, we are pumping fifty billion a week into the global economy and the International Monetary Fund is concerned about inflation in the Eurozone and the East Asian economies. We have the I.M.F. boss telepresent in three minutes, plus finance ministers from E.U. and China and representatives from ASEAN."

Zem is not really listening, he's thinking about Megan. He is wondering whether she will immediately accept the offer or if he will have to argue with her. Maybe he will need an inducement. A flower from the frangipani tree, maybe.

Zem enters the lobby, but instead of moving towards the Auditorium, he stops and the entourage halts immediately around him. He turns to Ollie who is the tallest duckling in the group. "So what do I do?" he asks.

Ollie has let go of his grumpy mood because he has found a way to get rid of Megan for a few days. He answers, airily, "It's really simple. Just say: *Megan I have been invited to a party and I would like you to come.*"

"What are you doing, Swede?" asks Erin, agitated.

"Anton is going to invite Megan to an oilman's party."

"What? Now?" asks Erin, exasperated.

"Iron while the iron is hot," says Zem, cryptically.

"Bullshit! Not while the President of the I.M.F. is telepresent," snaps Erin.

"And my iron is very hot, right now."

Erin takes Zem's arm and says, "Listen, Anton, I don't mean to put shit on your right hand, but do you really want to be taking relationship advice from the Swede?"

"What is that supposed to mean?" demands Ollie, angrily.

"What did you buy your wife on your first wedding anniversary?" Erin asks.

"A bio-plastic water bottle," says Ollie, as if that wasn't weird.

"See what I mean?"

"How about this," says Zem, "you guys figure out what to tell the I.M.F. I am inviting Megan to an oil party."

Zem moves away from the entourage. He walks through the lobby and swipes himself into the private quarters. Outside Megan's door he stands with his fist raised to knock but stops, aware of an unusual feeling. He finds himself confused and unsure whether he should proceed with his plan. He feels anxious that he is about to be face to face with Megan. It is a strange and debilitating sensation.

Then the door sweeps open, and Megan is standing right there. Zem is suddenly present to a flurry of colours and the delicious scent of coconut tanning oil accelerated by Megan's body heat and ethanol. Her brown eyes twinkle under the down lights in the hallway and her lips glisten with balm.

"Zemitheree," she says taking a step forward and wrapping her arms around his neck. She squeezes her breasts deliberately against his chest, paralysing him.

Zem feels like a lion cub gripped by the scruff. He notices the softness of her breast. Megan un-hugs him and places a kiss on his cheek. She asks sensuously, "Zemmy. Would you like to come inside for a quick daiquiri, say... Thirty-five seconds?"

"This is an unscheduled meeting," says Zem, taken aback by her amorous advance.

"We could trim it down to thirty seconds."

"I mean it could go longer," he says.

"A whole minute?" says Megan, enthusiastically.

"How long do we need?" asks Zem, confused.

"Well, it depends on what you had in mind," she says, theatrically, rolling her shoulder. "I hear you space boys go at the speed of light. But let's not go rushing for Uranus until we have had time to get to know each other."

Zem is unsure why Megan is using this funny voice and feels that he has neither the time nor the Earth training to adequately respond. So he cuts straight to the chase and says, rather formally, "I have been invited to a party and I would like you to attend."

"Are those Ollie's words?" asks Megan, suspiciously.

"He recommended them, yes."

"Can I offer you a more amorous approach?"

"Okay."

"How about this," she says. "Megan darling, it's been such a rush, what with saving the biosphere and all, I just can't get the little paddy shit to schedule the time to see you; but a fantastic opportunity has arisen for us to spend some quality time together... And then you say Ollie's bit."

It seems verbose, but otherwise, makes sense. "Okay," says

Zem, eagerly. "So will you come?"

Megan deflates, "You were supposed to say… Oh, it doesn't matter. Sure, I'll come. Where is it, in the Auditorium? Do I bring my own soft drinks?"

"It's in Huston, Texas."

"Texas? America?"

"Yes. It's an oil party."

"Oh, Anton, you surprise me."

"You called me Anton," he says, pleasantly surprised.

"And that won't be happening again, Zem!" she snaps.

"So will you come?"

"Well, I don't know. What sort of party is it?"

"It's an oil party. Lots of oil people."

"I'll need a new dress."

"Take a chopper to the clothes shop in Dubai."

"*Uh-huh?*" says Megan, suddenly interested. "You going to come shopping with me again. *Huh?* Remember how that ended up?"

Zem sees an angle for an inducement, and he adds, "You can take Ollie's credit card, so you won't have to spend your own money."

"I am starting to like this proposal," says Megan. She runs her finger around the knot of his tie. "Something else?"

Zem continues, "It has a half a million-dollar limit."

"Zemitheree, I want to eat you."

"So, that's yes?" Zem asks, hopefully, excitedly.

"It's affirmative with a big cherry on top, sexy man."

"So, is that yes?" asks Zem, still confused.

"It's a yes, Zemitheree!" Megan snaps. "Don't ruin it."

"Well, that's great. For the details, Ollie will fill you in."

"Oh, no he won't," says Megan, seriously.

"I have to go now."

"Of course you do, dumpling."

"Apparently, our program is causing inflation in the global economy," says Zem with a haughty smirk. "I have to go and sort it out."

"*Tut, tut, tut,*" says Megan, theatrically wagging her finger. "The world just wasn't ready for you, was it Zemitheree?"

Zem turns and walks along the hallway with Megan watching from her door. "Nice ass!" she calls out to him.

Zem swipes himself out of the private quarters and pushes the door closed behind him. He rests his back against the wall processing the discussion with Megan. How strange was that?

He walks quickly into the auditorium where the telepresence monitors are filled with human faces. The auditorium resonates with chatter and all eyes are watching Zem behaving oddly. He is puffing and grinning and distracted.

"How did you go?" asks Ollie.

"She said yes," says Zem, breathlessly.

"Great," says Erin, slapping him on the back and turning him to face the stage. "Ready to explain yourself to the I.M.F?"

"Okay, let's go. Oh…" Zem stops and turn to his men. "What does 'great ass' mean?"

Ollie shows a blank look.

Erin says, "It's a good thing, Anton, it's a good thing. Up you go now, mate." He shoves Anton towards the stage.

Zem steps into the center of the stage and looks up at all the people observing him. From the larger screen shines the face of an old man in his sixties. He has a forty-year career in banking and international institutions, but Zem is completely unprepared for him.

"Good evening Mr. Vorlov," says the President of the International Monetary Fund.

"I'm sorry," says Zem. "Do I know you?"

En-route to Houston

The introduction of Ollie's credit card dramatically changes Megan's perception of her job with Between Destiny. She makes daily trips to the vast retail precincts of Dubai and Abu Dhabi, and after a few weeks she feels like she has the general measure of them. The frustrations of her role as Zem's personal assistant are swept away in a blaze of bright lights, global fashion brands, and the palatial comfort of the largest shopping malls on the planet.

Finally, at the agreed time, Megan is ready to go to the party. The first leg of the trip to Huston is a chopper flight from Between Island at three a.m. Ollie comes to her door and is surprised to see a stack of bags, and even more surprised when he is forced to carry them to the chopper.

"Where is he?" asks Megan as she struts down the hallway wearing $4,000 leather boots, and noticing with stifled pleasure that Ollie is struggling to keep pace with her.

"What have you got in here?" he asks, panting.

"You gave me the credit card, Ollie," Megan says defensively. "Where's Zemitheree?"

"Anton is at the Greenhouse. He'll meet you on the plane."

"Who are we flying with?" Megan asks, not happy with the previous answer.

"Vorlov Airlines."

"What?

"Private jet."

"Suitable," says Megan.

The Sikorski chopper flies Megan and Ollie to Dubai International where Ollie transfers her bags into a Gulf Stream executive jet.

Megan feels like it is second nature to walk up the steps into the jet and turn to see Ollie struggling behind her with her bags.

Ollie stows her bags and says, "Anton will be here shortly."

"Thanks, Ollie." Megan opens her purse and retrieves a fifty-dollar bill. She tucks the bill into his breast pocket, saying, "Put that towards one of your green projects."

Then she turns to the interior of the jet. It has a similar fit out to Zem's helicopter. The fuselage is lined with white leather. There is polished walnut fittings and a large flat screen TV. There is a bottle of champagne on ice next in between two large leather couches. She pours a glass, and slumps down in a chair. In moments she is asleep.

When she wakes, the plane is in the air and Zem is in the seat in front of her. He has the appearance of a large statue: solid, powerful, unyielding; and yet he exudes warmth, and he is smiling gently, looking at her over a document.

"Where are we?" Megan asks. She rubs her eyes with the back of her hand and adjusts herself on the white leather seat.

"We are in the lower stratosphere," says Zem. "I like it up here," he says, softly, leaning forward to expand on his story. "We are eleven kilometers above the Earth and it's minus fifty degrees Celsius out there."

"Cool." says Megan, squirming in her seat. "I can't believe we're going to a party in a jet," she says. "I normally take a cab."

"Is it just us?" she asks, looking around.

"There is a pilot and a navigator in the front."

"So, we are alone?"

Zem smiles as he watches Megan nod off to sleep again.

When she wakes again, she sees in front of her a tray containing a most magnificent meal. It has fruits and cold meats, seafood, three types of fresh juice and a rich and complex aroma.

"Wow," she says, suddenly hungry. "This is a lucid dream."

"Breakfast with altitude," says Zem.

"Breakfast, alright. You not eating?" she asks in a perfunctory manner that justifies her to immediately tuck into the food.

"I have my Virid."

"What's in that stuff, anyway?" asks Megan, searching through the fresh fruit.

"It is micro-lichen in liquid form."

"Say what?"

"It's a composite organism made of algae and psilocybin fungus."

"So, you're tripping on Magic Mushrooms all the time?" Megan chortles. "That explains a lot."

Zem lets a wry smile slip. "Not tripping. Micro-dosing."

"Explains why don't eat human food. Like this, for example," Megan demonstrates by slipping a piece of mango into her mouth, and she watches Zem as she chews.

"Then I'd sleep and lose my Parrathean abilities."

"Is that it?" Megan chooses the next target for her toothpick.

"It would also heighten physiological and emotional propensities that would interfere with my mission."

"*Hmmm*," says Megan. She mulls this over for a little while then says, "I remember the first time you drank it."

Zem makes a quizzical expression, "Really?"

"Don't you remember, we set up the fish tank on the

balcony. You had to drink like a thousand litres, and you got really sick. You said it tasted like a seaweed milkshake."

"I don't remember that."

"You only remember the work stuff."

"I don't remember much of what happened before I drank the Virid."

"Do you remember throwing up on Toddy?"

Zem looks at his hands.

"Anyway," says Megan, that was what, six years ago?"

"My departure must have caused you emotional distress," says Zem with a tone that approaches humility.

"It did. A lot," says Megan, firmly. She punches the toothpick meanly into a small gherkin, as if it were receiving the punishment that Zem deserved. She says, "That little group of humans hung together for three years before you arrived. It lasted about three months after you left. And then poof. Toddy shacks up with this mole from Ingham, and Al, my brother, goes all space-cadet on hooch for six months, then starts a law degree. Go figure."

Megan is chewing and watching Zem thinking it through. She empathizes with him. What is he supposed to do? Really?

"It doesn't matter, Zem," she says.

"I think it matters."

"Well, let's say that it doesn't matter in the same scale as carbon in the atmosphere matters."

Zem nods gently. "True that."

"It's old. Just silly human emotion stuff," says Megan. She harpoons a cooked prawn and dips it in mayonnaise.

Zem raises a smile and sees Megan looking directly. She says, "You're off the hook, mate."

Zem sighs, feeling as though he had been holding his

breath during the conversation. He watches Megan eat and she looks up at him periodically, grinning in that seductive way that she has.

"I'd like to spend more time with you, Zem. If the schedule allows."

"I'd like that," says Zem.

"Really?"

"Yes, I would."

"It's not going to interfere with your work?"

"Of course it will. But fixing this planet of yours is a bit of an never-ending job, so..."

"A bit of R&R will do you some good."

"That's not necessary for a Parrathean."

"Maybe you can stop being a Parrathean for a while."

"I'd like that."

The Oilman Awards

The Oilman Awards is the gala event of the year demanding the most luxurious appointments. There are tuxedos and cocktail dresses from wall to wall, and crystal chandeliers overhead.

Zem and Megan mingle amongst the crowd ahead of the dinner ceremony. The long conversation on the plane has put Megan in high spirits. She wears stilettos and a shimmering blue designer dress. The silk gently caresses her skin making her feel amorous and the luckiest girl alive.

Zem seems ill at ease and Megan realizes that he has had very little experience with social events. "Always carry a drink," she says, handing him a champagne glass. "Maybe cover it with your hand like this, so no one can see you're really not actually drinking it." Megan's fingers adjust his on the glass.

"You look very..." says Zem, and then realizes, he doesn't know the word.

"What? Very what?"

"What's the Earth word?"

"You could try 'beautiful'. That would work."

"You look very beautiful, tonight," says Zem with an intonation that immediately makes Megan blush.

"Oh, wow," he says observing her face closely.

"What?" asks Megan.

"Your skin has changed colour and your pupils have widened," he says.

"You have just passed your first compliment," says Megan. "How did I go?"

"You duxed it."

A woman holding a tiny Chihuahua dog brushes against Zem and it flicks out its pink tongue to lick the back of his hand. Zem pulls away instinctively.

"He's a bit shy around dogs," says Megan to the dog's owner. "What's the little baby's name."

"This is Squiggle," says the woman.

"Squiggle. Oh, wow. Could I?" Megan reaches out and Squiggle squirms happily as the woman passes him over.

"A lesson in being human," Megan says. "Kiss Squiggle on the nose."

"Is that legal in Texas?" Zem asks. He is not sure what to make of this, but he does as instructed. He leans forwards and pecks the tiny dog on its wet nose. Squiggle goes crazy and Megan presses the Chihuahua to her cheek and beams at Zem.

Zem is mesmerized by the look of the pair of them together.

"*Une magnifique synergie*," says Zem.

Megan hands Squiggle back to her owner. "I love Squiggle. I want one." The woman moves away with Squiggle and Megan takes Zem's arm. She places a kiss on his cheek.

"You're so good with animals," she says.

"You're so good with humans."

A man in a tuxedo addresses the crowd from the doorway of the dining hall, calling for everyone to take their seats.

"Hold like this, so you don't lose me," Megan instructs, manoeuvring Zem's hand to thread through her arm. "Then we walk together."

"I like it," says Zem, and they move with the crowd towards the hall.

The hall is huge with dozens of tables laid in silver service.

Zem and Megan are shown to Wayward's table where there are gruff oil executives, Wayward's mates, and their adoring supermodel girlfriends.

"Looks who is here," bellows Wayward when Zem is shown to the table. "It's Mr. Vorlov, the Ukrainian from Dubai."

Wayward steps up from the table and approaches Zem. He is rotund with a red face and an aroma of peppermint toothpaste. He steps into Zem's space and peers at his face as he shakes.

Wayward says, "Now I have shaken your hand and looked into your eye. Sit down, Anton, enjoy the show." Wayward slaps Zem on the back and guides him to a chair.

"And who's this little peach you've brought with you?"

"This is Megan," says Zem, guardedly.

Wayward goes to take her hand but Megan steps back. She makes a forced smile in exchange for touching the oilman.

"A bit shy, this one. Definitely not a Southern belle," says Wayward. He makes his way back to his seat and announces, "Challenging industry, the oil business. Oh my! Can't build enough of them Hummers. Oh yes. Sit down, Anton! Sit the fuck down and enjoy yourself. You are amongst oilmen now. Petroleum oilmen that is."

Zem takes his seat with Megan to his side. "Are you okay?"

"I don't like your dinner host too much," she says.

"It was a mistake to bring you here. We'll leave shortly if it doesn't improve," Zem says.

Wayward starts talking again, and receives the adoring attention of his entourage, "Oil industry. Big challenges. Competition from unexpected places. Just want to reaffirm what a real oilman looks like! Oil is black folks, not green.

Speaking of green, we have a special guest tonight: Anton Vorlov." Wayward raises his glass to Zem and everyone toasts with him.

Zem raise his glass, "To the cream of the oil."

"Great to have you here, Anton. Or Atlas." Wayward pretends to whisper to a female companion, but everyone hears him, "Atlas. In-house name from his private island."

Wayward's drunken female companion leans to Zem, "Do you have an entire island for your privates, Mr. More-love?" She breaks into a peal of laughter and is joined by the other drunks at the table.

"Love your party, Tom," says Zem.

"What actually is your reason for holding the world on your shoulders, shifting destinies around?" asks Wayward.

"Change is as good as a holiday," says Zem, wittily.

"And what happens when you meet someone who is happy with the old destiny?" Wayward asks with a sinister tone.

Megan fidgets awkwardly, feeling the tension rise.

"Then we have many interesting things to discuss," says Zem. He feels Megan take his hand under the table. He looks to her and sees fear in her eyes. He doesn't want that. He needs to take her away from here.

Wayward claps his hands together loudly and announces, "Excellent answer, Mr. Vorlov. And in the tradition of my homeland, I insist that you try some of our Louisiana Creole Cuisine. You can't have a deep and meaningful with an oilman without it." Wayward holds a bowl of food to Zem, staring at him.

Megan gasps and grips Zem's hand tighter. He glances at her reassuringly. Zem takes the small bowl and observes the guests at the table. They are all looking at him expectantly.

Wayward pipes up and says, "It's a mix of French, Spanish, Portuguese, got some crab in there, bit of pelican, and a dash of light sour crude." The oilman is watching Zem very intently, observing his every move.

Zem looks into the bowl. It contains a thick soup with dark lumps in it. It has a rich spicy aroma. Zem fixes his eyes on Wayward and scoops the food into his mouth and swallows. Then he locks his mind into ensuring that he doesn't throw it back up again. "Delicious," he says.

Wayward watches him intently, waiting for a reaction. The tension is palpable with all of Wayward's people following their bosses lead, looking at Zem.

Then Wayward says, "I have seen what I need to see, Vorlov. Get off my table and take the bruised fruit with you."

Zem steps up from the table, his eyes fixed on Wayward. He takes Megan's hand and leads her through swiftly the dining hall without speaking. He marches her to an emergency stairwell and descends three flights of stairs. Megan struggles to keep up, her high heels clipping along at pace.

Zem sweeps through the door at the bottom of the stairwell into an alleyway at the back of the hotel. He takes three steps before buckling up and throwing up the creole cuisine into the gutter.

Megan flusters around him, patting his back as he retches. "He knew. He knew you shouldn't eat."

"I know," says Zem, sucking the vomit from his mouth and spitting the last of it into the street.

"Are you okay, baby?" she asks.

Behind them, the fire escape door opens, and four tough

guys step out of the building. They are dressed in leathers, like the bikers that Zem knew from Townsville. He sums them up immediately from the way they move, aggressive but undisciplined fighters.

Zem stands to his full height and wipes his mouth with his thumb. He takes Megan by the shoulders and physically moves her against the wall saying, "I feel pretty good now, Megan," then his voice turns severe, and he says, "Do exactly as I say. Stand here."

Megan is gripped with fear, and she watches as Zem turns to address the men who halt five paces away, "I'll say this once only. Leave now or you die here."

One of the men retrieves a metal bar from a long pocket sewn into the leg of his jeans. He taps it on his hand then launches himself at Zem.

Zem steps nimbly aside as the bar crashes down. He snatches the metal from the thug's hand, twisting it free. The man is jerked off his feet, tumbling forward. Zem slams the metal bar hard and fast against the side of his skull. The thug is dead before he hits the ground, the side of his head caved in.

Zem steps quickly forward and demolishes the other three men with a series of hard, blunt force traumas to the skull and neck. It is merciless, brutal and quick. Within seconds, the four men are reduced to bloody lumps in the alley way.

Megan pushes back against the wall, horrified. The first of the men lies at her feet, blood pouring from the side of his head.

She watches, mortified, as Zem adjusts the corpses and retrieves the wallets from their back pockets and tosses them her way. She shrinks as the bloody wallets slide across the concrete towards her.

"Take them," snaps Zem.

Megan looks around and sees a plastic bag in the gutter. She retrieves it and places the wallets inside, then shoves this into her purse.

One of the thugs makes a gasping noise and Zem rolls him over and looks into his bloody face. He grips the man by the throat and raises the iron bar above his head, "Who's man are you?" But the thug's voice box is crushed. He coughs up blood and expires.

Zem looks around the alleyway then steps towards Megan. She is motionless, holding her purse against her chest. He takes her hand and marches her down the alleyway.

Somber Return

Once the Gulfstream has reached cruising altitude, Megan exhales a long, deep breath. Her anxiety slowly declines, and she becomes present to herself, curled up in the thick leather chair under a blanket, facing Zem.

Zem is seated motionless, silently, observing her. His shirt is splashed with blood and his face is fixed; his eyes locked on Megan's. His heart is pounding, not from the fight, *per se*, but from the sense that he has to ensure that Megan's life is never endangered again.

It is very rare for Zem to feel out of control, and he has mapped out a dozen ways to improve security around him. And he is trying to think how best to act human around Megan. He remembers their discussion after the incident at the pawn shop all those years ago. He recalls how flustered she was at even the suggestion of violence. Now that she had seen him in full swing with all the gore that goes with it, he guesses that she will be out of her wits. So he doesn't interfere with her, just watches over her protectively as she processes the information.

"Are you okay?" he asks, eventually.

Megan swallows deeply and nods her head repeatedly, unconvincingly. Tears start to trickle down her face and Zem watches, captivated by the streams of water, human emotions given a physical form.

"What should I do, Megan, to be more human?"

"You need to give me a hug."

"What is that?"

Megan shifts off the chair onto the floor and rests her back against the fuselage of the jet. She opens her arms and beckons Zem to come closer. He sits next to her and she lays her head against his legs and holds tightly onto his hands.

Zem just complies with her, and sits there, motionless, listening to the sound of her breathing and the occasional choke as tears catch in her throat.

Cold Shoulder

Back on Between Island, Megan stomps off the chopper and along the jetty. Zem follows her but when he reaches her room, the door is closed. He knocks three times and waits but there is no answer. He looks forlornly at the door handle, listening intently, but there is no sound.

It is all very perplexing. He gave her a hug as she requested. Then after a period she pushed him away. And when they transferred to the chopper at Dubai International, she looked away from him the whole time and said nothing.

Zem moves away from the door and walks slowly along the hallway towards the lobby. Erin is there and a crowd forming around him.

"Anton," says Erin, hurriedly moving towards him. Zem can't face a crowd right now, so he turns, swipes back into the private quarters and enters his office. Erin follows him in. Ollie is there, asleep on the ottoman.

"Close the door, Erin," says Zem.

"You're back. How was it?" asks Ollie, rubbing his eyes. He sees that Zem is agitated.

"We have a problem," says Zem. He retrieves a package from his pocket. He tosses the bloody bag containing the four wallets to Ollie who catches it, examines it in the light, makes guttural squeak and drops it on the floor.

Zem says to Ollie, sternly, "We are attacked outside the hotel. It was a set up. These are the wallets of the men. I need documentary evidence linking them to Wayward. Get onto it straight away."

Erin enters the room and immediately Zem addresses him, "Erin, schedule a meeting with Directors. This organization needs a proper security division. We must prepare for war in order to avoid it."

"What happened?" asks Ollie.

"We were attacked."

"I mean what happened to the attackers."

Erin's phone rings and he takes the call. He listens intently, then says, "Send it through to the monitor in the Auditorium." He lowers the phone, his face ashen.

"Anton, there is bad news. Come quickly."

Zem, Erin and Ollie move quickly from along the corridor, through the lobby and down the slope into the Auditorium.

The Auditorium is half full and the crowd in there are chatting anxiously. One of the schedulers activates a remote control and plays a recorded CNN News story.

The image shows the fire raging at an industrial facility. The camera sweeps past the Between Destiny logo on a gate. There are ambulances, emergency teams and paramedics moving about. A gurney comes into view, and there are gasps from the people in the audience as they recognize the man. It is the chief of the Algae Division, one of Zem's inner team.

The announcer says, "The blast, thought to have been caused by a faulty methane valve, tore through the algae farm at eleven this morning. Among the dead was Between Destiny's Chief Scientist."

There is a noise of sadness and anger from the crowd. Zem studies the news broadcast intently. "Roll it back," he says to the scheduler with the remote control. The news story runs backward at three times speed.

"Stop there. Play it now," says Zem. The news footage plays and Zem steps closer to the monitor staring at the screen. He continues to instruct the man with the remote.

"Stop. Go back. Stop. Play. Get ready to pause it. Pause."

"There," says Zem, pointing to a spot on the monitor which shows the long plastic tubes in which the algae fuel is grown.

He turns to the people in the auditorium looking for a face, but he can't see it. He turns to Ollie and Erin, but he is not seeing what he needs to see. He is looking for one of his team members, the old guy who runs the algae farm, but he can't see him.

Zem announces out loud, "Where is Terrence? We need non-return valves there. Right there. That's why the whole lot blew up. It is not designed against sabotage."

Zem is met with a wailing noise from the auditorium. He looks up in surprise to see people getting up from their seats, their faces reddened from sadness. Zem is perplexed, he looks down to Ollie who is just shaking his head in resignation.

"What?" asks Zem, perplexed.

A heavyset middle-aged woman bowls down the aisle towards the stage. Ollie and Erin cower as she approaches. She pulls to a halt at the stage edge and addresses Zem with a sharp, harsh tone. It is Cassie, head of human resources, the exhausted human whose job it is to replace the people who quit the team.

"Mr. Vorlov," she barks. "May I characterize the staff of Between Destiny, in a few words."

Zem looks at Ollie for direction, but his right-hand man gives him up.

"Don't look at me," Ollie says. "I have been warning you for years."

Cassie continues with her blunt tone, "Your staff are

overpaid and over-worked, and while yours is a critically important program that we all dearly love, there are many competing priorities such as friends, family, cultural holidays, rest, sleep and so forth."

Zem is dumbstruck. He has heard this argument many times before, mainly from Ollie, that taking a holiday is more important that preventing the destruction of the living systems of the Earth. He is as confused as usual and now has one of his own senior members berating him. He shows a blank look, and she continues.

"One second we learn that twenty of our staff are killed in an industrial accident including one of the inner-circle – who was probably the person you were looking for just then – and next minute there's a design fault to be fixed and jolly pip, off to work we go as if nothing had happened."

"What would you have me do?" asks Zem, honestly.

"A mourning process might be appropriate."

"How long would that take?" he asks.

Suddenly, Cassie's demeanour changes from angry to something much worse. She picks up a pen from the table in front of her and throws it full strength at Aton. It misses him but clatters against one of the monitors behind him.

Then Cassie turns on her heels and storms up the aisle of the auditorium which by now is all but empty. She gets to the top of the aisle and shouts, "Today, even I quit! Effective immediately!"

Zem looks astonished. He glances at Ollie and Erin who both look like animals trapped in headlights.

"What just happened?" asks Zem.

"You H.R. manager just quit," says Ollie.

"We'll hire a new one," says Zem.

"Wrong answer, Anton," says Erin, shaking his head. "Wrong answer."

Gun Boat

Two weeks later, on Ollie's suggestion, a professional photographer arrives on Between Island to take a group photo of the inner core of Between Destiny. Of course, Zem can't understand why such a photo would make a difference, but he is going along with it, anyway.

Zem had made a special trip to seek Megan's thoughts on the matter and she spoke to him for the first time since the trouble at the oilman's party. The deal was clinched when Megan agreed it was a good idea.

On the day of the photo-shoot, Megan is in good cheer. She has cleverly managed to convince Erin that Zem's schedule should permit at least thirty minutes before and after the photo-shoot, to really cement the celebration.

Megan is frocked-up beautifully and smelling gorgeous, having discovered the synergy between the perfumes of the Middle East and Ollie's credit card. Even Zem is in high spirits as he is progressing a new plan to cut Wayward out of the deal with Brenton Prest.

The inner core of Between Destiny comprises about a hundred people. They are mostly executives from various industries and all firmly committed to the restructure of the global economy spearheaded by Anton Vorlov and his vast reservoir of wealth.

It is a warm day underneath the frangipani trees in the main garden of Between Island. The crowd forms and Megan demonstrates her people skills by encouraging the people in the crowd to shuffle closer.

Zem senses her high spirits. He has spoken little to her since the incident with the four men getting killed, but he feels as though today she has moved past that.

She takes his hand and moves him to the center front of the crowd and he allows her to force him to squat so that the body of his group is above and behind him. She won't talk to him directly, but every time he glances at her, he sees that she his looking at him and then she averts her eyes.

The crowd is almost set and the photographer calls for attention. He looks through his view finder and shifts the camera so that the group is in the center. Above them are the branches of the frangipani trees, behind them the flat waters of the Gulf and in the distance a boat with a spray of white water on its bow.

The photographer grunts. The boat shouldn't be there but it spoil the photo. He looks up from the view finder and motions for the group to shuffle in some more.

Front and center is Megan and Zem, side by side. Zem wiggles a little finger, and Megan and takes hold of it.

"I am sorry I have been such a cow," she says.

"I wish you hadn't had to see that violence."

"If you hadn't done that to them, something terrible would have happened to us."

"It was a bad situation, but we did okay."

Zem looks to Megan and for the first time since the night of the oilman's awards, she holds a gaze into his eyes for a long beat. Megan suddenly looms large in Zem's senses. Her perfume synergizes with the aroma of the garden. He feels her fingers gripped around his little finger. It is as though there is a torrent of energy passing between them through that tiny physical connection of skin.

"Come on, come on," shouts someone, theatrically from the crowd behind, but Zem is thinking the opposite. Time is shooting past him at such speed that it makes his head spin. Slow down, slow down, he thinks.

Zem hears the camera going *click-click-click* as the shutter reels off three frames. He feels Megan's fingers grip tighter on his, like some strange earth ceremony that is turning him upside down.

Click-click-click.

The photographer looks up from the viewfinder. He says, "The lady in the red dress, can you move in a bit. That's good. Saying cheese."

Click-click-click.

For Zem time is moving at close to the speed of light. Time is not an infinite quantity for him, and he knows that being with Megan will not last for ever; his time with her is running out.

"Are you okay?" asks Megan, looking his face. But Zem is far from okay. He is as 'un-present' as he has ever been, deep inside the rabbit hole of his own psyche. It is dark in there, with the sensation of endless falling, and the feeling that he may never see the light again.

"You look beautiful today, Megan," he says, slowly, delivering his Earth compliment with more conviction and sincerity that any of the millions of words he has spoken since he fell into Alligator Creek.

Megan's eyes glisten as moisture forms there. A smile breaks across her face, changing the contours of her skin like the way shifting tectonic plates force low mountains from flat plains.

Click-click-click.

The cameraman looks up, frustrated, that boat is coming closer, looming larger and larger in the viewfinder. He can see more detail of the vessel now: the man standing on the bow behind the metal structure.

"In a bit. In a bit," says the photographer, gesticulating, trying to block out the speeding boat. He grunts, frustrated and makes a slight adjustment to the camera to hide the boat behind one of the subjects.

"And saying cheese one big time."

"What is it with cheese?" asks Zem. He watches as Megan's smile spreads so far it seems as though it will touch both sides of her face. The smile forces against her lacrimal glands and a little blob of moisture appears there. Zem marvels that humans grow tears both when they are happy and when they are sad. No wonder he gets so confused around them.

The *click-click-click* is now accompanied by another sound, the pattering noise of small hard objects flying a high speed through the air and into the foliage of the surrounding trees. Zem looks up in a daze and sees frangipani petals shattering above him. They burst into yellow and white fragments, like wet fireworks. He sees leaves exploding into violent spatters of green. He has seen this before and he becomes instantly present.

There is a scream from behind and above. And the piercing whistle of hundreds of high velocity rounds zinging through the air. And the hammering sound as bullets slam into trees, walls and human flesh.

A burst of red right in front of him! Megan's hair wraps around his face as he pulls her against him and slams her onto the grass, smothering her with his body. Bullets impact and all hell breaks loose in the garden. There are screams and yells and the crowd breaks and scatters, chaotically.

The maelstrom of fire ceases as the speed boat turns away from the island, and races towards the open waters of the Gulf at full speed.

Zem's team are stunned and bloodied. Some crawl across the grass. Others clutch themselves, crying. There is chaotic movement as people rush for the safety of the building and someone's foot slams into Zem's head. He feels hands grabbing him under the arms and hauling him to his feet and he sees that Megan is gone. She is gone! He sees that the hands gripping him are those of his two closest aides. He casts Ollie and Erin aside and they fall on the grass.

Zem makes a military appreciation of the situation. He scans the seaway and the beach and assess the terrain is open and exposed, his own force is helpless and floundering, and the enemy is in retreat.

The threat is gone for now. He stands to his full height sucks in a huge chest full of air and bellows his only Earthly request, "WHERE'S MEGAN!?"

Zem turns, scans the carnage of his island garden: trees fallen, branches dashed with blood, people crawling across the grass with open wounds.

"WHERE'S MEGAN!?" Zem's voice pounds the island like naval artillery.

WHERE'S MEGAN!?" his voice booms, like a ranging shot; and then the artillery fires for effect, "WHERE'S MEGAN!? WHERE'S MEGAN!?" WHERE'S MEGAN!?"

Ollie shouts, "She is here. She is here," but Zem cannot hear for his own distress.

"WHERE'S MEGAN!? he bellows, his voice higher now, something human choking in his throat.

Then Ollie slaps Zem square across his face and points to

Megan, crouched in the doorway of the building, her eyes like a frightened cat's. She is calling for him, but no words are coming from her mouth.

Zem races to her, sweeps her from the floor into his arms and runs inside with her. He bursts through the campus, through the lobby, down the aisle in the auditorium and to the back of the stage where it is dark and quiet and safe. He lowers her to the floor and lays there with her. Curled up with her. Holding her tightly.

"Nothing will happen to you," he says, desperately, his face nuzzling into her neck, her hair falling around him like fiery wool. "Nothing will ever happen to you while I am on Earth."

Megan places her hands the back of his head and pulls his face deeper against her skin. "It's okay, baby," she says. "It's okay. It's okay."

Bottomless Truth

Later that day, Ollie is watching as paramedics move a wounded man on a gurney along the jetty towards a waiting boat. The wheel jams in between the planks of the wooden pier and the victim grimaces as the gurney is tugged free. Ollie shakes his head morosely. He looks up to see Zem marching towards him with a burly man, one of the security contingent that has been flown at short notice to the island.

Ollie reacts anxiously to Zem's approach, he holds his hand up and talks rapidly, "Whatever you do, Zem, do not say to me: 'we lost ten people but that's alright because we can get ten more' just don't say that, okay?"

"It's okay, Ollie. I was going to say I want you to direct the mourning process. Tell Erin everything is cancelled until it is undertaken to appropriate Earth standards."

"Earth standards," sneers Ollie. "Listen to it. Tell me, Zem, what is appropriate mourning where you come from?"

"It lasts about ten years, but you don't really notice it," says Zem. "And Wayward has an informant on this island. I need him found, right now."

Ollie looks dumbfounded. "Are you kidding? Where do we even start to look?"

"Get the photographs. Tell me who isn't there. I'll be with Megan."

Zem marches away towards the campus. He swipes into the private quarters and knocks gently on Megan's door. Eventually, he hears a click as she activates the lock from inside and he turns the handle and enters.

She moves back to the couch where she is curled up in a ball. The drapes are closed, and the room is dark and cool.

Zem closes the door quietly behind him and sits down on the floor next to her, with his back against the couch.

"Were many people hurt?" she asks softly.

"We lost some good people today," says Zem.

"Are you okay?" she asks.

"I am fine," he says unconvincingly, then thinks it through. Zem is fine, in that he is occupied with wracking his brains to figure out how to get his program back on track. It seems senseless to allow the deaths of ten people to stall a program that seeks to save eight thousand million of them. But how does he explain that to a human? And he is fine except that he realizes that Megan has become a liability to his project. He thinks about her too much.

"I shouldn't have brought you here," Zem says.

"You didn't, Ollie and Erin did," Megan replies, quietly.

"I mean, I feel as though you shouldn't be here."

Zem hears Megan sniff close to his ear and he strains to hear any other sound from her. He is hoping to be able to deduce her thoughts so that he can have advanced warning of them. Was that an appropriate Earth question, given the circumstances, he wonders?

"It's not safe anymore," he says.

"Do you want me to go?" she asks with a voice as flat as Gulf on a calm day. "You can tell me the truth."

The truth, thinks Zem, is a very human concept. What is the truth? Megan being on the island is interfering with his capacity to transform the global economy, there's a truth. Her leaving will ensure her safety assuming a further attack. But her leaving means that he will have no way of knowing she is safe in the other place. The truth is that he shouldn't be thinking about one human when his mission is all of them.

The truth, is a circular question; a bottomless pit filled with multivariate equations that stretch into infinity, like the decimal places of pi. The truth is he just wants to know that she is safe and to hell with all the rest of the humans.

Then Megan says quietly, "Thanks for protecting me," and she touches her fingers on his neck, just below his ear. She draws a little circle with her fingertips, "I will do what you think is best."

Zem is paralysed by that tiny fingerprint. The truth is unfathomable. What should he do? How long should he think through all of the options. What would Erin advise in this situation? *Think about it later.*

The Mole

Later, Zem is in his office with Erin and Ollie. Spread across his desk are the prints of the photographs taken that day. They have been cross-referencing these against the manifest for the photo-shoot. A single name has become apparent.

Erin says, "The only one who isn't there is Peter Turn. We checked his phone logs, but nothing suspicious. But the technicians found that he had been making VoIP calls to an IP address in Louisiana. They dug into that and found it was the gateway server to Wayward's laptop."

"Plus this," says Ollie. He pushes a driver's license across the table. It shows the face of one of the four men dispatched by Zem in the alley way. "That's Peter Turn's brother."

"Revenge," says Zem, gravely. "Where is Peter now?"

"On the mainland with the others."

"Erin, take my chopper. Bring him back here straight away. Tell him we need him for a special project. Make something up so he is not suspicious. And be discrete, no one else must know."

"Your chopper pilot will know," says Erin.

"My pilot is good for it," growls Zem, his voice raising. "And this is no time to be questioning me. Do you understand?"

"I get it," says Erin, feeling hairs rise on the back of his neck.

"Then go, now," snaps Zem and watches as Erin departs.

Zem turns to Ollie. "Now, Ollie, draw up a cheque for a million dollars made out to Peter Turn. I want you on standby for when our new friend arrives. Do it now."

Zem departs the office and returns to the beach where he joins the head of security and walks with him around the island until he sees his chopper arrive.

He moves to the jetty and meets Ollie walking toward the chopper. "Do you have the cheque?" he asks, curtly.

"Yes," says Ollie.

"Okay. Get in the chopper."

Zem opens the door of the cockpit and talks to the pilot. When he is done, he steps into the back of the chopper. Ollie, Erin, and Peter Turn look at him silently.

Zem shakes his head and says, "Erin get out."

Erin is mighty glad to be free from the chopper and he watches from the edge of the helipad as it alights.

Inside the cabin, Zem presses his tongue against his lip and looks at Peter Turn. Turn is mid-forties. He is an economics professor who specialises in non-fractional currencies and steady state economics. He looks nervously at Zem from the corner of his eyes.

"How long have you been with the team, Peter?" asks Zem.

"About three years?"

"*Uh-huh.* Do you like your job?"

"It's a great job."

"What do you like about it?"

"I have been promoting the zero-growth economy since I learned about it in my graduate degree. You pay me handsomely to actually implement it."

"Well, that's good news, I guess," says Zem.

"And who would you recommend for taking your place if you suddenly disappeared off the face of the Earth?"

Turn has trouble enunciating the words, "I… I work with woman called Terri. She is good."

The helicopter purrs across the Gulf and Zem observes Turn's eyes flicking nervously from place to place, as though he were looking for a way out. He fixes Turn with an ominous grin and observes that Turn gets quite chatty when fearing for his life.

Turn says, "Erin says that you have a special project. Can you tell me about that?"

"That's exactly right, Peter. Thank you for reminding me." Zem glances across the cabin and sees that his resistance to interrogation techniques are affecting the Swede as well.

"I like your concept of cabbage and stick," he says.

"It's carrot," says Ollie.

"A cabbage is bigger than a carrot, Ollie," says Zem, leaving no room for debate. "Give me the cheque."

Ollie removes the folded piece of paper from his pants pocket and hands it to Zem.

Zem holds the cheque up in front of Turn's face. "Read it," he instructs.

Turn's mouth suddenly goes dry, and he gulps hard, trying to bring saliva onto his tongue. "It's a Between Destiny cheque for one million dollars."

"Who is it made out to."

"Peter Turn."

"And you are Peter Turn, aren't you?"

"Yes."

"For now, at least," says Zem.

"I don't understand," Turn stammers.

"That's your signing bonus for taking on a new job."

"What is that?" he asks, hoarsely.

"You are now a double agent, spying on Wayward for us. That's the cabbage. You know where this is going, don't you, Pete?"

"The stick?" he says, gulping.

"Yes, the stick," says Zem and then rapidly slides open the door of the chopper. The air-conditioned cabin is instantly blasted with the hot, wet air of the gulf and chopper exhaust carrying the sweet smell of fresh popcorn.

Hearing the door slide open, the chopper pilot follows his instructions and drives the helicopter nose down towards the sea. This creates the sensation of uncontrolled falling in Turn and Ollie, as well.

"I don't normally eat," says Zem as the chopper plummets towards the sea surface. He rolls the cheque into a ball, places it in his mouth and starts to chew.

Both Turn and Ollie are astonished to watch Zem chomp on the piece of paper until it is rendered into a small, soggy mass.

The chopper comes to within thirty feet of the sea surface and then rapidly straightens up. Zem very calmly reaches out and grips his fingers around Turn's trachea.

"*Fuuu*—" Peter instantly grips hold of Zem's forearms, but he can do nothing to relieve the agony of his windpipe being crushed. He struggles for a second, then goes completely still, staring at Zem, his skin pulled tight across his face.

Zem looks across at Ollie. He is hyperventilating, his hair waving around madly as the air bursts through the cabin.

Zem rolls the chewed-up paper to one side of his mouth allowing him to say, "Bear with me, Ollie. It gets a bit messy from here on in." Then he turns his attention back to Turn.

Foremost in Zem's mind is that this man was responsible

for the attack on the island in which Megan could easily have been harmed or even killed. His Parrathean sensibilities are to do whatever is necessary to have the man provide information to prevent further attacks. However, humanness floods his thinking, and it expresses as a lust for violent revenge.

He smiles at Turn and then spits the mashed-up cheque at him. It ejects rapidly from his mouth and slams into Turn's eye. Turn winces and Zem methodically slams the back of his hand against his face, once, twice, three times. Each blow forces an anguished squeal of pain and Turn writhes. His cheeks burn bright red and his head spins. Blood comes from his nose and finds its way into his mouth.

Zem raises his voice and screams, "I'll tear the skin off your face if you deny me!" He growls, like a rabid wolf, "*Hrrrrr. Hrrrrr. Hrrrrr.*"

Across the cabin, Ollie, feels his balls shrink. He scrambles onto the seat trying to escape.

Peter gags, gripping his hand on Zem's forearm as he is dangled out of the chopper. Above his head, the blades thrash the air, and just below the hard sea surface flashes past at three hundred kilometers an hour. The whining of the chopper engine bounces off the sea surface.

"Where is he!?" shrieks Zem, "I will eat you up! I will eat you alive! What's he doing!?"

"Leave me. Help. Help me," shrieks Turn, panicking and choking.

"You are coming on board the team," shrieks Zem, shaking Turn out of the chopper by the trachea.

"Okay, okay, I'll do it!" shrieks Peter, terrified.

Zem drags Peter inside and slaps one more time across his

face. Peter starts crying, whimpering, clutching his face, trying to crawl away. His eye is swollen, and he has blood all over his face.

Zem grabs him by the ear and hauls him up.

"What were you thinking?" bellows Zem.

"I am conflicted," shouts Turn.

"*Uh-huh.* Tell me more."

"You killed my brother," weeps Turn, trying to protect his ear from being pulled off, "You killed my big brother and now he is gone."

"The arrow of time has only one direction Peter Turn. So you are working for me now. Tell me about Wayward. What's happening in his world?" Zem lets Turn slump to the floor and cocks his fist.

"Don't hit me," screeches Peter and scrambles across the cabin to where Ollie is standing on the seat, his back pushed up against the fuselage.

"My brother was just an idiot who did stupid things," he wails. "When I learned how he died, I called Wayward, I visited him, and I told him I wanted revenge on you."

"Revenge on me?! Well, I am having my revenge on you! Tell me something I want to know."

"He's having a function on his rig," stammers Peter. He holds his arm up to protect his face; tears are flooding from his eyes.

"His rig? What is that?"

"He's resurrected the Deepwater Horizon, the rig that blew up in the Gulf of Mexico. He's obsessed with it."

"Where?"

"It's moored in the Mexican Gulf."

"Who will be there?" Zem bellows. He glances over to

Ollie and sees that Ollie is leaning in, listening intently.

"All of them. The consortium that oppose your algae projects," says Peter, whimpering. "They will all be there,"

"Who is all of them?" asks Ollie.

"He's aligned twenty major oil companies against you."

"When is this meeting?" asks Zem.

"The anniversary."

"Of what?"

"The Gulf of Mexico Oil Spill."

Zem looks at Ollie calmly and nods at length. He pinches Turn's trachea and hangs him out of the chopper. After fighting and scratching for a few seconds, Turn goes perfectly still holding onto Zem's forearms and trembling.

Zem turns to Ollie and smiles warmly. He says, "The trouble with torture, Ollie, is you can never really be sure whether the victim's information is true or something that they have made up to stop the torment."

Ollie is motionless, pressed against the wall of the chopper, looking first at Zem, then to Turn's bloodied, contorted face, then back to Zem.

"So what do you reckon?" asks Zem.

"Reckon?" Ollie stutters.

"I have a warm feeling about what I have just been told."

"Warm?"

"Yes. So, do we keep him on the team, Ollie?"

Ollie looks into Zem's eyes and makes a long gulp noise through his parched throat.

"I won't be around forever, Ollie. You are going to have to make some hard decisions in my absence."

"You are in command now," says Ollie.

"I most certainly am. And if you leave it to me, I will

execute him right now."

"Execute?"

"At this speed, he will be dead on impact with the water surface. Sharks will get his body. He will just disappear."

Ollie looks out across the vastness of flat blue sea screaming past. He feels that they are invisible to the rest of the world. He thinks about the man grimacing in the gurney and the others also killed. He thinks about the enormous scale of Between Destiny's task and how this one man stood in its way. And how he could so simply just disappear.

Ollie says, "I think we let him go."

Zem loosens his grip on Turn's trachea. The steady state economist tumbles into the slipstream.

Big Swim

A few nights later, Megan is sitting up late in her little garden looking at the sea when she hears a noise of something being dragged on the sand. There are many new, strange noises since the security contingent has been deployed on the island, but this one is close-by, and it stirs her interest. Even though it is dark, she can just make out the shape of Zem dragging a small dingy down the beach.

He pushes the small boat into the water, steps in, deploys the oars and starts to row in the direction of the neighbouring unoccupied island.

Megan is intrigued. She drops her sarong and walks to the water's edge. Zem is drifting out of view, and she can just hear the last faint noises of the oars splashing.

Without thinking, she wades into the into the sea and starts swimming in the direction of Zem and his boat.

She swims overarm for a distance before she tires, then changes to breast-stroke which allows her to keep her head up and navigate towards the island. A hundred or so meters through her swim she looks back to see Between Island with its garden lights illuminating the foliage. Up ahead is darkness. She suddenly feels vulnerable, not knowing how deep the water is below her, or what might be considering her as a meal. A chill spreads through her body and she halts, treads water, and contemplates her fate. She is faced with the choice between the swim back to Between Island, a known distance, clearly lit, or the uncertainty of swimming into the darkness. She feels something touch her toe and wave of panic flashes through her. She turns and swims quickly back to her beach.

Calling Home

Zem pulls the dingy up onto the beach of the sandy patch neighbouring Between Island. From the floor of the dingy he retrieves his special bag, the Transit Pouch. He walks in the dark across the sand and illuminates a flashlight. In the middle of the island, there is a pale brown tarpaulin, and he pulls this aside to reveal a concrete stairwell leading down into a cavern excavated in the sand.

The cavern is circular, about four meters wide, and with walls of sandstone. The ceiling is white concrete. Zem wedges the torch in the sand floor, pointing upwards. He opens his bag and retrieves the remote control on crystal meth and activates it.

Seconds later there is a swirl of blue, a loud crack and Zem is face to face with Music, Verten and Torreth.

"Hello Zemitheree," says Music, softly. "How is Earth treating you."

"It is causing me some concerns, right now," he says.

Music smiles knowingly and this makes Zem feel comforted. He is with his people again. But his comfort doesn't last long.

"There have been changes to our plans," says Torreth, abruptly. "We have to bring you home early."

"Early. How early?" asks Zem, disarmed.

"The ship will be passing through the teleport event horizon in twenty-six thousand seconds," says Verten.

"That's… That's less than a month away," says Zem, exasperated. "My work here is not complete."

"Then you will need to wrap up the business with the oilmen very quickly," snaps Verten.

"Can you complete the oil business in a short time?" asks Music.

Zem grits his teeth and looks away. He turns his face back to his Parrathean audience.

"I will need to use the Oil-man's Hammer," he says.

"I have already stated that I will support the use of the Hammer," Music says. She addresses Torreth and Verten, "I am expecting no objection from you."

Torreth and Verten shoot each other furtive glances but they are silent on the matter. Music takes this as quiet consent.

"Use your judgment, Zemitheree, but seek the counsel of the wise humans. Remember, it is not our job to kill humans to save humans; only they can make that decision."

Zem nods gravely, then he says, "There is one human who I would like to bring back to the ship."

"No, Zemitheree," says Verten, abruptly.

"I think that it would be good to have a human onboard," Zem protests even though he knows it is futile.

"Zemitheree, I will remind you of what you already know," Verten snaps. "Humans are strictly prohibited from our ship."

"But why?" he pleads. He sees Music observe him with a sad smile, but she lets her male companions continue.

"Why?" repeats Torreth, exasperated. "Have you learned nothing about humans during your time amongst them? In every cell of their bodies are genetic sequences that code for their own personal destruction, the destruction of their fellow beings, and that of the biophysical systems on their planet. That's a pretty good reason."

Zem feels cowed by this response, and he bows his head.

Torreth continues, "We cannot risk that these sequences get into the Parrathean gene pool. You will bring no humans back to the ship, Zemitheree! Palau?"

Music watches Zem struggle with this rebuke and Torreth raises his voice, "Palau!?"

"Palau," says Zem, begrudgingly.

"So make preparations for your departure," snaps Torreth.

"Destroy the Virid," says Music calmly, "And create an engaging story to explain why you won't be around."

"I will stay," says Zem, non-committedly.

"Whatever for?" says Verten.

"There is one human who is special to me. I do not want to leave…" Zem stops part way through his sentence.

"Leave 'her', perhaps, Zemitheree?" says Torreth.

Zem bows his head, feeling as though he has transgressed for even thinking such a thing.

"She is special to me," he mumbles.

"Special to you? More special than your own people?"

"It is hard to explain but…"

Torreth implores, "Zemitheree, there are eight thousand million humans on Earth who would be committing collective suicide if not for you. Suddenly you want to change your own destiny on behalf of one individual. You are Parrathean. Whatever are you thinking?"

"Are you still drinking your Virid?" asks Verten, as if this were the explanation for Zem's disobedience.

"Yes, I am still drinking the f**king Virid!" snaps Zem.

"What did he just say?" asks Verten.

"It doesn't translate well into Parrathean," says Music. She turns to her two male companions and says, "Verten, Torreth, please leave me to speak with Zemitheree alone."

"Maybe you can talk sense into him," says Torreth.

"Good luck to you Zemitheree," says Verten.

The two elder Parratheans depart the auditorium and Music remains. She watches as Zem digests the new information.

"I am sorry that we had to cut the mission short."

"I know how it works. You don't control the ship."

"You are exhibiting emotions that are not of your race, Zemitheree," says Music.

"Does our race actually exhibit emotions, Music?" he asks.

"Yes, we do. In our own way. I admit, somewhat less dramatically than our human friends."

Zem breaks a smile that spreads across his face. The tension in him fades and he makes a little laugh. He looks up at Music and sees that she shares his grin.

"They have this ritual with a thing called an egg sandwich," he says, barely able to contain his laughter. "And when they capture images of themselves, they talk about this milk product called cheese."

Music withholds the desire to laugh. It even looks as though she is happy for a few moments before Parrathean gravitas overcomes her.

"Save your Earth stories for when you are back with your own people," says Music.

"Yes," says Zem, sombrely. "When I come back alone."

Dry Hump

Megan sits on the beach on Between Island, staring into the night. She thinks over her swim in the warm, black water. She is concerned that she launched into the venture with such aplomb, and annoyed that she didn't follow it through.

She spends some time in her own recriminations until she hears the noise of one of the new security guards crunching along the beach. Instantly, without thinking, she stands and walks into the sea. She dips her body beneath the surface and swims under water. Beyond the reach of the Between Island architectural lights, she breaks the surface as silently as she can. Then she methodically swims into the darkness towards shadow in the stars that is the neighbouring island.

This time, her swim is purposeful, fearless and swift and she soon finds herself bumping into the sandy shallows. Close by, along the beach, she can see a faint glow of light reflecting off Zem's dingy.

Megan stands and looks around the island illuminated only by starlight. A little way in the distance she sees a narrow strip of light and she walks across the sand towards this. She approaches and finds an entrance way, a flight of steps leading down into a cavern.

There is light at the bottom of the steps and the sound of talking that she recognizes as Zem's language.

Megan descends stealthily to the bottom of the stairs and peers around the corner. There is Zem, laughing with the woman again. The laughter to last only a few seconds before the conversation goes cold and then shortly ends. The woman's face fades and the blue bubbles disappear. Then, all that is left is Zem standing in the sandy cave, illuminated only by the torch.

Megan suddenly feels vulnerable. It is so quiet that she daren't move in case she be heard and discovered. And she daren't speak aloud for fear of startling Zem, and who knows what would happen them.

But Zem doesn't move. He just stands there, staring at the far wall where Music's face had been. It is silent, very still. His body is motionless, as though he were a pillar of sand extending from the ground.

Megan becomes present to her own breathing but is unable to move from her position except to raise her hand to her mouth. Zem continues to stare at the ground, now making the occasional gasp as though he is having powerful realizations.

He lets out a long sigh, thinking through the discussion with his people. If he were all Parrathean, it would be straightforward, but he has some human in his thoughts now and this slows him down and adds other elements for consideration.

For example, when and how should he tell Megan that he has been instructed to return to his ship. How does one express that to a human without causing unnecessary emotional pain. Indeed, how does Zem himself accommodate that information? Zem feels that he is inadequately trained in Earth matters to deal with this question. He suddenly wishes that he had taken the often-repeated advice, to learn to be more like them.

This is so hard, Zem thinks, searching the roof for an answer. What would Erin advise in this situation? *Think about it later.* That always seems to work.

Zem begins to move. He turns his attention to his

shimmering teleport bag on the floor. He places the remote-control device inside. Then he retrieves the torch and makes towards the stairs.

Megan is ahead of him, having made her getaway as soon as he started moving. She reaches the water's edge and stops, suddenly terrified at the prospect of entering the sea again. Her conviction that the waters are safe has completely gone. Or maybe she just doesn't want to travel back to the island alone.

So she just stands there, feeling as though she were on the edge of a cliff and unable to move away. A torch-light shines around her.

"Megan," says Zem, surprised.

"Hi Zem," she says, squinting into the light and waving with one hand.

"How did you get here?"

"Swum."

"Swum? Is that a word?"

"I swam. I saw you and I just wanted to be…" Megan shields her eyes from the light and Zem directs the beam to the ground.

"Did you see me?" he asks, cautiously.

"Not really," she lies. "Is everything okay, Zem?"

Zem turns off the torch and allows his vision to adjust to the dark. From the empty sand island, the dim lights of Between Island are visible gently illuminating the foliage and key architectural features of the campus. Seven kilometers distant the lights of Dubai burn and twinkle like a bright smudge on the horizon. And far above, the Milky Way softly pulsates, the photons from the distant conglomeration of stars appearing white and wispy.

"We should go back," he says.

"Can I come in your boat with you?" asks Megan, cheekily.

Zem lightens up at the thought of Megan swimming alongside the dingy as he rowed. "Sure," he chuckles.

Then he thinks, what an extraordinary situation this is. Standing in a vast blackness with little drips of light coming from different directions. There is no immediate danger on the beach and yet a sense that he should be somewhere else.

"Maybe you'd like to drive," says Zem, light-heartedly.

"You want me to row?" asks Megan, smiling at the idea.

Zem drags the dingy into the water and illuminates the torch, shining it onto the seat to make Megan's entry easier. He smiles as he watches her step into the boat and nearly capsize. Eventually, she is seated in approximately the right place, and she draws the oars close.

"Do you need guidance?" asks Zem.

"I will tell you if I need help," she says. "I mean, if a spaceman can row, it can't be too difficult."

Once Megan has established the proper function of the rowlocks and is ready for her first stroke, Zem pushes the boat into the water. He steps nimbly onboard and sits on the back seat and turns off the torch.

He leans back and watches the Milky Way pulsing at him. He hears the sound of splashing as Megan tries to propel the boat. The city of Dubai moves around in a full circle as Megan hacks the sea surface with the oars. "There is something wrong with this dingy," she says.

At every butchered attempt to sink the oar into the sea, Megan throws a spray of water into the air. Every stroke unleashes pale green flashes of light as iridescent marine algae flare up then fade away. When Megan is able to strike the oar into the water and pull the dingy against it, the tiny glowing plants spin off in eddies from the edge of the blade under the surface.

"How am I doing?" she asks, breathing heavily.

"You are doing great," says Zem.

He trails his hand in the water watching the tiny lights sparkle around his fingertips.

"This is such a magnificent planet," says Zem, dreamily. "It would be such a shame to let the oilmen burn it up."

When the dingy finally crunches into the sand on Between Island, Megan helps Zem pull it onto the beach.

"That was awesome," she says and slaps him gently on the shoulder. Then she wraps her arms around his body and hugs him, looking up at his face. He doesn't move her away and she feels as though she has captured him. His body is so large and strong. She wants him to kiss her. She desperately wants him to care about her in a physical way.

Zem looks down at Megan. He sees her mouth is open, her lips moist and she has a dreamy look in her eyes. He wants to engage with her in the same way, but he doesn't know the rules. Plus, the question comes back to Zem's mind, and it paralyses him. How does he break the news to her that he has been sent home early? Should he tell her now?

"Did you hear me talking on the island," he asks.

"Sure I did," says Megan rubbing her breasts against his chest, trying to get a rise from him. "It was all Zebbedee this and Zobbobbly that. I don't speak a lot of paraffin wax, you see."

"Did you call me Zobbobbly?" asks Zem, amused by Megan's demeanour. He gently places his hands on her back and notices that her skin is pliant from having been in the water. Her body is warm, and firm and he can feel her gyrating her hips so that her crotch rubs firmly against his thigh. He is comfortable holding her like this but concerned that he has to tell her about his early departure. Should he tell her now?

Megan is panting quietly, and her pupils are very wide. Her breath expels in a rhythm that times with the movement of her hips. She shifts her hands onto his buttocks.

"Do you know what this is called?" she asks him, dreamily, pulling herself harder against his leg.

"What's it called?" he says.

"This one is called horny. It's been growing for a while now."

"Really, how long?"

"Oh, about six years." Megan shifts her body, pushing her pelvis against his. She doesn't get the uptake that she wants so she shifts back to his hard thigh.

"Are you with me on this?" she pushes against his leg.

"I am not sure," says Zem. "What are you doing?"

"It's a puppy dog thing," she says, building up a head of steam.

"Like Squiggle?" asks Zem.

"*Huh?*" she murmurs, distracted.

"Like the little dog in Houston."

"*Hmmm?*" she asks as she grinds her crotch against his thigh.

"You had me kiss its nose, remember?"

Megan gasps, "Say that again."

"What?"

"Kiss his nose."

"Kiss his nose?" asks Zem.

"*Oooh*. One more time."

"Kiss his nose."

Megan gasps loudly and her finger push hard into Zem's butt. She lets out a long moan and her knees go weak. She lets Zem take her weight while she swoons and hangs in his arms breathing heavily, her eyes rolling.

"Are you okay?" asks Zem, confused. "Do you need a doctor."

"I just saw one," she says breathlessly. She looks at the tall, strong spaceman holding her in the dim light of the garden.

"Oh, Zemitheree," she says, coming down from her rush. "That was very nice." As she recovers, she comes to her feet and stands back a pace.

"*Hooo!*" she sighs. "Sorry about that. I got a bit human on you, there."

"It's okay," says Zem, not really sure what just happened.

She takes a few more steps back, "I guess I just need to be okay that I am the personal assistant to a platonic space man. But, thanks for that, anyway."

"Megan, there is something I want to tell you."

"That's okay, Zem," she says. "You don't have to say anything." She turns and walks towards her apartment.

Zem watches her go. He scratches his head feeling at once a sense of confusion and lost opportunity.

Gone AWOL

Next morning, Megan wakes late and stumbles to the table on her beach with a coffee. Ollie is stomping along the beach and when he catches sight of her he approaches and asks anxiously, "Have you seen Zem?"

"I last saw him last night about eleven," says Megan, smirking at Ollie's obvious discomfort. "Has he missed something important?"

"Nothing much really, just a phone call from SecGen."

"Reschedule," says Megan smugly, sipping her coffee.

"Do you know who SecGen is?"

"How would I possibly know that, Ollie? I am just the underutilized personal assistant who doesn't get to assist personally." Megan adjusts the lapel of her dressing gown and Ollie notices the gilt lace and delicate fabric. It looks exceptionally expensive.

"Do you still have my credit card?" he asks.

"So, who is SecGen?" asks Megan, feigning interest.

"Oh, just the Secretary General of the United Nations who is working with us to the massive climate talks coming to Dubai."

"He'll call back."

"That's not really how diplomatic relations work."

"Well, aren't you in the shit, Ollie. The right-hand doesn't know where the rest of the body is."

"Nicely put, Megan. Thanks for that."

"No worries, Swede. You want a coffee?"

"No. I am actually freaking out right now. Let me know if he turns up, would you? We've got a--"

"Tight schedule," interrupts Megan.

She watches Ollie march off along the beach and chuckles to herself that he seems to be looking for Zem in the bushes. Where would Zem go she wonders. It is hardly that much of a concern; of all the people in the world, he is one self-sufficient man. Plus, she got a bit last night, and she still has the credit card, so what does she care?

She looks across the flat waters of the Gulf and sighs. Another day in paradise with nothing to do. Nothing to do? Hell, she thinks, I am a ten-minute chopper ride from Dubai.

She showers, dresses, confirms that she still has Ollie's credit card in her purse. Then she calls the pilot of Zem's helicopter to take her to a shopping mall.

At the landing pad she addresses the pilot, "I am going to hang in Dubai for a while. Would you ask Mr. Vorlov to call me when he gets back to the island?"

"Certainly, Miss Megan," says the pilot.

She steps into the Sikorski helicopter and in fifteen minutes steps out of the chopper pad onto the roof of a globally significant shopping precinct where she commences to wring some love out of the Between Destiny credit card.

At noon, she stops shopping and treats herself to a Margarita. At 2.30, she stops for another. And another at five, as per regulation. By seven she has found her way to the Burj Al Arab, the world's most luxurious hotel, and learned that her credit card is warmly received there.

By midnight, Megan is plastered, and dancing with an Italian man in the nightclub on the ground floor of the hotel. She stumbles out of the nightclub when he makes amorous advances towards her and spends the best part of an hour drunkenly playing with the huge slate fountain in the lobby of the hotel. By three a.m. she is asleep in a hotel suite that costs

$15,000 a night.

Midday the next day, Megan is eating a banquet in bed and checking her mobile to see if there are any calls; which there aren't. She thinks this through and wonders how long her luck will last. So she makes an executive decision to live it up until either Zem calls, or the credit card runs out of love.

After the banquet, Megan walks to the lobby of the world's most luxurious hotel and sits down with the travel agent, an elegant African woman with braided hair and pink lipstick. Megan likes her instantly, and she asks a light-hearted question.

"What's half a million as a percentage of twenty trillion?"

"Is that long scale or short scale?" asks the travel agent.

"What's the difference," asks Megan.

"Six zeros."

"How do you know that?"

"I used to work in a bank in Zimbabwe," the African lady smiles. "You get used to dealing lots of zeros."

"So how many zeros are there in a trillion?" asks Megan.

"I'll assume we are talking short scale because you are speaking English. So there are twelve zeros."

The travel agent starts tapping numbers into the calculator.

"But my calculator doesn't go that high," she says.

"*Hmmm*," says Megan, feeling like the answer has eluded her.

"I think that half a million is a tiny proportion of twenty trillion," the travel agent says.

"You think so?"

"It's tiny."

"You are right," says Megan. "Half a million is trivial."

And with that pressing concern neatly handled, Megan is

free to start booking trips. She gathers up a collection of brochures and sorts them into order of preference and then commands her new friend to get to work.

She books herself onto a camel ride in the dunes; a helicopter trip to the dead center; a ride on the Jumeirah Scarer waterslide; a swim with the sharks at Atlantis Resort, and an hours snow skiing in Mall of the Emirates. She organizes these events keeping in mind the way that Erin structures Zem's itinerary, taking note to ensure sufficient travel time between each venue. The difference being that her itinerary allows plenty of time for quaffing daiquiris and taking long lunches, manicures, pedicures facials and massages.

Once Ollie's credit card has been punished some more, Megan returns to her palatial room and dresses appropriately for the first of her adventures. She steps out of the hotel wearing a rabbit-fur waistcoat, Elton John-esque sunglasses and green leather boots. She generously tips the limousine driver when he delivers her to the first venue.

Everywhere Megan goes she meets nice people to hang with and when they ask her what she does for a living she makes up fanciful stories. And no matter how audacious the lies, the people believe her. She is just projecting that kind of energy.

Five days pass before one of the two triggers occurs. She wakes to the sound of her mobile ringing. It is Zem's number.

"Hi Zem," she says, disconnected.

"Hi Megan," he says. His voice sounds flat, like he was emotionally drained; like all of a sudden he had emotions to be drained. "Where are you?"

"Oh, I am in some fancy hotel somewhere in the Middle East living large on magic pudding credit card. What about you, Zem? Where are you these days?"

"I am in my office. Are you alone?"

"Alone," says Megan, sitting up in bed, suddenly annoyed. "Am I alone? You know what Zem, I am as alone as I have ever been in my life right now. How about you mate? You alone?"

"I am alone," says Zem, gravely. "My people are billions of kilometers away and I haven't seen them for over six Earth years."

There is a long pause during which time Zem's emotional state wins out over Megan's. Eventually, he says, "I would really like to see you."

"Where have you been?" Megan asks, meekly.

"I had some oil business to attend to. It is done now."

Zem's voice is flat and yet completely compelling, "I would like you to come home, Megan. Would you come home, please?"

"Okay, Zem. I'll come home."

"Where are you?"

"I am in the Burj Hotel."

"I'll send the chopper right away."

Megan In Excelcis

Wearing all-white, Megan steps onto the platform on the top floor of the Burj hotel. Ahead of her, poised on the edge of the building, the helipad watches over the city of Dubai. The sky is vast and blue. Thick, aviation contrails crisscross overhead as though the atmosphere was being ripped apart to reveal a puffy white material beyond.

A long, red carpet extends straight and true towards a flight of white stairs, vivid against the sky. The emotional relief at hearing Zem's voice has made her light-headed, and Megan walks, trance-like, towards the helicopter landing area.

From the sky, Zem's helicopter descends. Its immaculate skin glistens in the sunlight and the profound music of its beating wings reverberates through her body. An outpouring of sweet-smelling exhaust engulfs her, the combustion products of algae biofuel. She sees the pilot turn his head and acknowledge her with a subtle nod. He is not wearing sunglasses today and she looks through his piercing, blue eyes and sees his deep into his mind. At that moment, Megan becomes enlightened.

Suddenly, all Earthly sensations fade away, and she feels as if her entire being 'sublimates' – turns instantly to vapor. Then, every thought, every heartbeat and breath compress into a tiny point. The physical structures that comprise her body interfere with their own shadow, annihilate, and send out a single photon of white light.

Megan is *in exelcis*.

The chopper's wheels touch down on the helipad and the mighty noise changes intonation as the machine no longer needs to thrash the air to stay aloft. Megan approaches the great metal beast, unafraid. A uniformed porter moves toward her. He places her bags on the deck and reaches for the door. Chilled, perfumed air from inside the cabin pours over her as the door slides open. The porter pushes her bags into the chopper and then offers her his hand as she steps inside the luxurious cabin.

Once seated on the white leather, Megan observes the porter bow, with his hands together, as if he had been blessed to have assisted her. She raises a smile, and he slides the door closed.

"Hello, Miss Megan," comes the voice of the pilot, a sound as solid and dependable as the helicopter itself. The chopper alights, and Megan feels gravity shift in her stomach.

As the Sikorski moves away from the incredible hotel, Megan is reminded of visiting Zem in the Greenhouse on her first day. She is on her way to see him, again. However, in this instant, there is no anxiousness. Instead, she has the feeling that, after a very long time, things have finally come good.

Coming Home

From the cabin of the Sikorski, Megan sees Zem standing on the perimeter of the helipad. She observes him looking intently in her direction and feels that there has been a shift in him. It is as though he too has found enlightenment during their absence.

She stumbles out of the helicopter, into his arms. The sensation of his embrace is like a hit of morphine, and she clutches him tightly, pushing her face against his chest. They hold each other as the hot air of the helicopter exhaust bursts around them like an aromatic hurricane. For Megan, the feel of his arms wrapped around her is more present that the turbine engines winding down in a long, descending whine.

Eventually, she lifts her face. Her eyes are rimmed with red and glistening. Zem places a kiss on her mouth and holds it there longer, much longer, than Megan thought possible. When they break from the kiss, Megan feels incredibly calm.

"Let's walk along the beach," says Zem. "It's a bit hectic in the campus right now."

"What's happening?" Megan asks, calmly.

"Between Destiny is learning how to get by without me."

"How's Ollie going with that?" she asks with a chuckle.

"Ollie is not a happy hen, right now."

"You mean happy chicken," says Megan, laughing.

Zem takes her hand and turns with her toward the jetty. As they walk, Megan moves her free hand across her body to take hold of Zem's forearm. He pulls to a halt and embraces her again, squeezing her tightly against his body.

Zem says, "When I got back to the island and you weren't here, I nearly went out of my mind."

Megan hears the tension in Zem's voice. "I am right here, baby," she says gently and strokes her hand on the back of his head. She looks around her, feeling overwhelmed by the intensity of the light and wanting desperately to be somewhere dim and private. She breaks the embrace and says, "Come on."

Megan leads Zem quickly along the jetty and onto the beach. They walk through the sand to Megan's apartment. She pulls a key from her purse as she approaches the door.

Inside it is quiet and cool. Zem slides the door closed behind him and pulls the drapes closed. Then he halts there, looking at her directly.

For a few moments they just look at each other, in the manner of two wild animals just before they clash. Megan is stunned that she is suddenly in receipt of something that she had taken six years to conclude was not possible. And for Zem, Megan is an entirely new suite of sensations that make him feel desperately hungry, vulnerable, and aroused. The dim room invokes the sensation of a Palaeolithic cave – cool and safe. For a moment longer they look at each other and then they come together like hungry beasts.

Megan pulls back, holding Zem away from her, her fingers pushed against the side of his head. Zem wears a look that she remembers seeing on the first day in the shack at Alligator Creek.

"What if the unhappy hen comes knocking?" Megan asks, thinking ahead.

"I gave him the day off."

"You are so clever," Megan says, breathlessly. She pushes her mouth against his and feeds on him.

She pulls back, panting, her face flushed. She looks into his eyes as she gently gyrates her crotch against him. Her familiar pleasure.

"I haven't had a drink for five days," says Zem. He places his hands on her buttocks and pulls their bodies together, firmly.

"I can tell," says Megan, breathlessly. "How is that for you?"

"I am a little tired," says Zem. "I think that's the word and…"

"And…?" she asks, expectantly.

"*Ummm.* I think the right word is…"

"What word?"

"Ready," he says.

Get Out!

Next morning, Megan wakes and finds herself looking dreamily at the ceiling, feeling a sense of exhausted bliss. She lets out a long sigh, and drifts back into sleep again. Except that there is an irritating noise, the sound of an anxious Swedish man banging on the bedroom window and calling her name.

She grunts, sits upright, and looks around the room, disoriented. She sees Zemitheree fast asleep next to her. The sight of him lying there, motionless gives her a sense of ease and the frustrated Scandinavian man slips from her mind.

Then Ollie raps on the window again and shouts, "Megan, wake up!"

"*Urrgh!*" she steps out of bed and drapes an expensive gown around her shoulders. She walks into the lounge and slides open the patio door. Ollie is still standing at the bedroom window with his bony knuckle poised to rap again.

"Oy!" she snaps.

Ollie scurries over to her wearing a worried look.

"What do you want?"

"I am looking for Zem. Is he with you?"

"He's sleeping."

Ollie has a conniption that Megan finds fascinating to watch. He seems to do a weird dance, almost like he was high on a cocktail of amphetamine and nerve gas. "Sleeping? You are kidding me," he rumbles.

"He had a big night," Megan says with a sly grin.

"You have to wake him immediately," Ollie stammers.

"That's just not going to happen."

"We have the Secretary-General of the United Nations in

seven and a half minutes to talk about the big climate talks. It's been on the schedule for weeks."

"Well, you go and sort it out, Chooky. you are on the big bucks."

"Are you kidd--"

Megan closes the sliding door and pulls the heavy drapes across them. Then she moves the edge of the curtain aside just a fraction to observe Ollie. He stares at the ground for a time then turns despondently and walks to the beach.

Megan returns to the bedroom and sees that Zem is awake now. She stands in the doorway looking at him lying there, the sheets pulled back exposing his chest and his belly.

"That was Chooky," she says. "I sent him away."

"I have to go," says Zem, abruptly.

"Go?" asks Megan, dropping her gown and stepping onto the bed. "You aren't going anywhere, soldier," she says.

She straddles him, sitting on his belly, pinning him to the bed. She grabs hold of his wrists and moves hands behind his head, then leans down and kisses his mouth.

When she rises, Megan feels Zem's eyes beaming into hers. There is pain in there.

"I have to go back to the ship," he says.

"Ship?" she asks, disarmed. "What are you talking about?"

"My mission has been cut short. I have to go back."

"What?"

"I am sorry, Megan."

"Are you making this up?"

Zem shakes his head in remorse, watching her face.

"Well, why are you telling me this now?" she stammers.

"I found out on the night we were rowing."

Megan suddenly tears-up. She puts her hand to her face.

"Why did you tell me now?" she weeps.

Zem is lost. Seeing Megan like this makes him feel wretched. Words suddenly pour out of him, "I didn't know when the best time was," he pleads. "I tried to tell you that night, but I couldn't. And I figured I couldn't not tell you like last time. So, I didn't know when. It just came out."

Megan sits upright and wipes her face with the back of her forearm. She is radiating heat and anger, "F*k it!"

Zem raises his hand to her face, but she swats it aside.

"I am so over crying about you Zemitheree," she snatches her gown from the floor, "Well, you turned into a real man in big hurry, Zemitheree? One night on the job and you are on your way. Well, get out then!"

"What?" Zem is dumbfounded.

Megan whips the covers aside. "Get out of bed you lazy bastard. Now! Out! Out! Out!"

Zem comes to his feet and stands, naked, not knowing what to do next. Megan makes it easy for him.

"GET OUT!" she swooshes him out of the bedroom into the lounge, and she keeps barking and swooshing until he is out the back door, stark bollock naked. Megan slams the door behind him and locks it.

Zem raps on glass the a few times before becoming present to his situation. He looks behind him and is relieved to see that the beach is empty although there is the sound of a helicopter approaching the island. Zem doesn't know much about Earth women, but he knows he not getting back inside Megan's room anytime soon.

He clutches his hands to his groin and shuffles out to the beach. He turns towards his quarters and scurries across the sand quickly. Arriving at this apartment he tries the handle of the patio door, but it is locked. Then he sees the drapes pull aside. Erin and Ollie look out at him, stunned. Zem raises a hand from his crotch and waves hello then rolls his finger signifying: open the door.

The door slides open and Zem enters. "Thanks lads," he says, moving past. "I just have to nip in here and get some clothes."

"Anton, what the fuck is going on?" protests Erin.

Zem rummages in a cupboard and returns wearing a pair of boxer shorts. He steps into a pair of suit pants.

"*Ummm.* I don't really know the word for it," he says, zipping up his fly. "I know you are a bit light on, Ollie, but Erin do you know anything about women?"

Erin stares dumbfounded at his boss hops around putting on a pair of socks. "What I meant was, what the fuck is going on with this organization?"

"It's in good hands," says Zem, unconvincingly.

"You skipped on meetings with SecGen," moans Erin.

"Reschedule," says Zem, pulling on a shirt. "Think about it later. You have lots of idioms. *Fuck, I don't know, whatever.* That's my new favourite."

"Anton just swore," says Ollie, stunned.

"About time, too," says Erin. "And what do we say to the U.N. Boss who you have just snubbed. We have 70,000 delegates showing up in Dubai to finalise the energy transition plan, and you are supposed to be organising it."

Zem is dressed now, jocks, socks, shoes, pants, and a shirt. He is about to step into the hallway to placate Megan when Erin shouts at him, "What are we supposed to do, man?"

Zem observes Erin and Ollie standing there, looking for answers. His closest Earth advisors are suddenly of little consequence to him. "It's not my job," he says, plainly. He receives just blank looks from the Irishman and the Swede. "This is not my planet, Erin. At some point, the humans will have to choose their own destiny. I have a new mission. You guys will be fine."

"A new mission?" asks Ollie.

"That's Parrathean for getting laid," Erin says.

"Tomorrow," says Zem. "Call a full executive meeting. Everyone. Midday. In the Auditorium. I have an announcement." Then he enters the hallway and walks towards Megan's door.

Humble Apology

In the hallway, Zem knocks on Megan's door and waits. And waits. Eventually, she pulls it open and stands back, her arms folded, her eyes on the carpet and her face all scrunched up in anger and disappointment.

Zem closes the door behind him quietly. He wants to embrace her but feels that it would be inappropriate. "I like acting like a human," he says, light-heartedly.

"Acting like an asshole," says Megan abruptly. "What does it mean you have to go?"

"Just like when I arrived. A flash of light and I am back on the ship."

"Can I come with you?" she asks, humbly.

The truth of the matter is that humans are banned from the Parrathean ship to prevent human D.N.A. entering the Parrathean gene pool. How do you explain that to your Earth girlfriend? That's an imponderable question, so Zem tells a good old-fashioned Earth lie, "You would never survive the teleportation process."

"And why can't you stay?"

Another question that Zem cannot answer truthfully, "I don't know when the ship will be close enough to allow me to return. I miss my people. I have to go home."

"Well it's just so messed up," says Megan, despondently.

Megan asks one final question, and it is hard for her to enunciate. She sniffs, wipes her nose with the sleeve of the expensive gown. "How long?"

"About two and a half weeks."

Megan wipes her eyes, "Well aren't I a dumb bitch?" She slumps on the couch, looking at the floor. She says, "Lesson one in being an Earth chick, never fall in love with a spaceman. You just know you are going to be disappointed. So what are you going to do, Zem?"

"Do?"

"Yeah. You going to spend two and a half weeks hanging with Erin and Ollie playing save the planet?"

"No. I am quitting formally tomorrow at noon."

"What about all your projects."

"I'll hand them over to the team."

"Shit," Megan is taken aback. "Ollie is going to handle SecGen," she chuckles, cruelly.

"You know about SecGen? I am in big trouble over that."

"Then what are you going to for the next few weeks?"

"I just want to be with you, Megan."

"Is that your conviction?"

"Yes."

"What will we do?"

"We could just hang out here," Zem suggests.

"I am a little bit over this gilded cage. Maybe we could go out somewhere?"

"Well, I am a trillionaire with projects all over the planet and a private jet. Maybe we could go and check some of the projects."

"Like the monkey project?" Megan asks, lighting up.

"Yes. The Gorilla's in the Congo. And the reforestation project in the Pyrenees. You can still ski up there. The geothermal project in Vanuatu. We could go see the volcano."

"Megan claps her hands excitedly, "We could fly Vorlov Airlines."

"First class! And everywhere we go," says Zem, extending

his arm across the room as though surveying the extent of the whole planet, "We punish Ollie's credit card."

Megan shrieks with excitement and leaps onto Zem, wrapping her arms around his neck and her legs around his waist. She kisses him on the mouth. He wants to speak so he pulls his head back and looks intently into her eyes and says, "But you have to let me go, baby, I am only here for a little while. You understand. You have to let me go."

Megan observes him somberly, and thinks it through. She makes a resigned sniff and tells him, "I know, Zem, I know. Spaceman has to fly. I knew that the moment you stepped out of the bedroom in that ridiculous old dressing gown. This boy is going to annoy me, pleasure me awhile, break my heart and fly away. I am ready for you."

"Then let us revel in the short time we have together, Megan. Let us fill every waking moment with adventure and fun."

"And shagging," whispers Megan, "Don't forget that."

"We will do it all," says Zem.

"We humans have an expression," says Megan. She places a kiss on the tip of his nose and says, "The light that burns twice as bright... Oh, I can't remember how it goes. But I am way ahead, with you Zemitheree. I am way, way ahead."

The Announcement

The next day at noon the executives of Between Destiny fill the Auditorium. There is none of the typical buoyant atmosphere and chatter. Today, just sombre whispers.

Zem takes the podium, "This room contains your planet's best hope of integrating human interests with the needs of your natural systems.

"My role has been to help you move from one destiny to another. From a future with a collapsed biosphere, toward the Verdant Age, deep into the Long Future. Stick to the plan and you are good to go for a Galactic Year. You have 230 million years ahead of you. All that was missing was a plan, some cash, and an institution. You have that now. Ollie has known all along that my role was finite, and today I am announcing my permanent departure, effective immediately, from all duties with Between Destiny. To quote the former head of H.R. and many former employees: I quit!"

There is a noise of astonishment and chatter from the people in the crowd. Ollie is gob-smacked. His mouth hangs open, speechless. He knew it was coming, but now it is formalized.

Zem continues, "Between Destiny has a detailed operational plan, plus the human and financial resources to accomplish its worthy mission. I am very confident to hand over my role to Ollie." Zem extends his arm in Ollie's direction and everyone in the room gets to observe the tall Swedish man who has suddenly turned quite pale.

"It has been a great pleasure to work with you over these years. Good luck to you all and goodbye."

Zem walks off stage and the people in the crowd are

stunned and confused. They talk out loud and argue.

Ollie meets Zem in the doorway. "You can't just quit."

"Ollie, I have been watching people quit this organization from the day we started it."

"Sure, but maybe you could give some notice. A decade would be good."

"It is not my planet, Ollie. And I am out of time, I have only a few weeks left before I have to go. I want to spend the rest of my time Megan. Just allow me that, Ollie."

Ollie stutters, "I can't be you. I can't work 24 hours a day."

"Then set your own schedule. You are the boss." Zem holds Ollie's shoulders in his hands. "You will do just fine."

"What about Wayward? How will we get the algae oil across the line with him in the way. He has put half the world's oil companies against us."

Zem nods gently, remembering that he has not briefed Ollie on this point yet. "Come to my office, Ollie. Bring Erin."

Deepwater Horizon

In his office, Zem retrieves a CD disk from a drawer and slides it into the computer. A video starts. Zem adjusts the monitor so that Erin and Ollie can see. He turns on the computer speakers, "Ollie has seen a bit of this, but you haven't, Erin. I have a dark side."

"A dark side?"

"It's really dark," says Ollie, shifting uncomfortably.

Zem scrolls through the video to an appropriate starting place. "Where was I those five days?" Zem asks rhetorically. "I was clearing a log jam in the Gulf of Mexico. Here we go." Zem hits play and rests back, watching the video.

The video is cut from images captured from the helmet cameras of a squad of a dozen gruff looking men.

"Who are these guys?" asks Ollie.

"Way back in the beginning," says Zem. "I was helped by men who rode motorbikes. Some of them has special forces backgrounds. This cost me five million out of petty cash, by the way. I didn't get a receipt. Sorry."

"You spent five million cash on bikers?" asks Erin, astonished.

"We got an exceptional ecological return on investment," says Zem. "Here, look."

The video shows the bikers from Townsville stripping off their colours and donning military uniforms. Then, the men assemble in fast inflatable zodiac boats. The zodiacs zoom across the water at night and blue cylume sticks illuminate the soldiers' faces. In the distance, a large structure looms into view.

"What is that?" asks Ollie, leaning into the monitor.

"That's Wayward's rig," says Zem. "Deepwater Horizon. It
blew up and sank in mile-deep water in 2010. He resurrected.
It's moored way out in the Gulf of Mexico. He's converting
it into a private resort."

The video shows the zodiacs pull-up under the rig. Some
of the soldiers disembark and climb the steps carrying
satchels. Others kit-up into SCUBA gear and roll backwards
into the water. Under the water, the soldiers scrub barnacles
off the concrete hull and affix black boxes there. Hundreds
of them. Above decks, other soldiers similarly attached boxes
to key pieces of infrastructure.

"What are they?" asks Ollie.

"Explosives. With a special fuse so they so they all go off at
once."

"Serious business," sighs Erin.

With the explosives fixed, the soldiers return to the zodiacs
and zoom away into the night.

"So, this is where it gets interesting," Zem says. "Wayward
invited all the holdout oil firms to a party on the rig. He's got
the entire C-Suite of petroleum executives that are resisting
the energy transition. Talk about low hanging fruit. We
picked up this video feed from their livestream."

The video shows what looks like a function room, albeit
one built into an oil rig. Glamorous showgirls serve booze
and canapes to hundreds of oil executives. There is a
commotion as Tom Wayward steps onto the stage.

"There he is," says Zem, tapping the monitor.

Wayward leans into the microphone. "Get these girls out
of here," he says. "Come on, snap-snap. Time for men's
business. Notwithstanding that we have some female oil
executives in our midst today. Good evening, ladies. We are

indeed a modern industry. Moving with the times."

Zem scrolls through Wayward's speech which seems to go on for an age before he gets to the good bit.

Zem turns up the volume, "You have to hear this"

Wayward says, "There are some who would say that a low carbon future is upon us, and the petroleum industry should be shot dead, like a pelican. This room contains the last hope to fight the greatest challenge ever faced by the petroleum industry."

"Is that Wayward?" asks Ollie. "He looks drunk."

"When you get close to him," says Zem. "He smells like toothpaste."

"You'd love him, Swede," jibes Erin.

"Up yours," Ollie grumbles.

"Listen to his speech," says Zem. He adjusts the speakers to better hear.

Wayward continues, "Today, I announce the *Petroleum Industry Transition Taskforce*. The PITT will lead the petroleum industry to the low-carbon future of *our* choosing. Over the next thirty years, we plan to lower the amount of carbon in the Earth's crust in a orderly, just and affordable manner. Each of you will play a part. So let's salute a low carbon future of our own design."

There is a sound of cheers as the oil executives raise their glasses in a rowdy vote of confidence in Tom Wayward. Then the video feed cuts off, and the screen shows white noise.

"What just happened?" asks Ollie.

"Well, that's when the explosives went off."

"And then what happened?"

"The rig went down to the abyss, taking the PITT with it.

And the best part is, we ran the catering, so we got all the innocents off the rig in a chinook before it went down."

"We ran the catering?"

"One of our companies came in with the lowest bid."

Zem hits the button on the computer and the CD ejects. He holds the disc up and wiggles it in the air, saying, "Handled." He squeezes the disc in his palm until it shatters, then drops the shards into a trash can next to the desk. "The lawn has been mowed, gentlemen. The energy transition can proceed."

Ollie and Erin look at each in muted shock.

Zem observes his two men contemplatively. He wants to continue to support them, but more than that, he wants to be with Megan. He extends his hands and shakes with Erin and then Ollie.

"I have to go now," he says.

Around the World

For Megan, the next two weeks pass in a blur; a potent combination of a spaceman, a Gulfstream Jet powered by algae biofuel, and the magic pudding credit card.

First stop is the Congo and a long trek through the forest and the cold mist to see the mountain gorillas and meet the families who protect them. Then they fly to the Pyrenees to see a million trees being planted. Then the chilly air of the Pyrenees is swapped for the humidity of the South Pacific and another trek up a mountain. This time it is to see a volcano shooting orange lava into the sky and to meet the people who run the machines that make electricity from all the excess heat. After the volcano of Tanna Island, they spend a few days out of Port Vila on a sailing boat.

By this time, Megan has come to terms with the fact that Zem is only around for a little while, and for the most part, this notion is far from her mind. But periodically she remembers, her chest constricts, and she finds herself counting how many days remain.

She is on the deck of the yacht looking across the sea. Zem has his head in her lap, with a hat over his eyes. Megan frets about how the final few hours will pass and how she will cope. Then a Humpback whale blows a mist of spray into the air and the crew of the yacht shout and point, and she looks up to see the great beast lying on its side waving a huge white fin at her. In an instant, the thought of Zem's departure leaves her mind and she engages in the magnificent spectacle of a whale at play.

However, a day later, in an empty second, the heavy thoughts return. Her chest feels tight and the thought of something that has not yet happened makes tears come to her eyes.

As the itinerary turns closer towards returning to Between Island, the pangs of anxiety and sadness become more frequent. She doesn't speak of this to Zem. If she did, he might tell her that he has the same thoughts flashing through his mind. Every day, at times he least expects. And the physiological sensation is the same. A tightness in the chest and feeling of anxiety and sadness. Pre-emptive grieving.

Eventually, the Gulfstream jet touches down at Dubai International and Zem and Megan walk across the tarmac to the waiting helicopter.

At the helipad on the island, Megan watches as Zem communicates with the loyal helicopter pilot. She stops and watches the exchange with a sense of foreboding. He talks to him in a different manner, less formally. Then he does something she has never seen before; he shakes the pilot's hand. Shaking his hand goodbye.

Megan turns and runs along the beach, tears flooding from her eyes. She knows that Zem's departure is imminent. As she runs, time speeds up around her and the last few hours of her time with Zem's pass in an instant.

New Schedule

Zem follows Megan to her room but finds that he is locked out again. He is now sufficiently Earth-savvy to know that he is not getting back in anytime soon. So he completes the few duties left to him on Earth. First thing is to empty the Virid from the tanks in the sunroom next to his office. He lets the green fluid flood onto the floor and hoses it down the drain where it soaks into the garden beds.

Next, he tracks down Ollie who is now the difficult one to see because he is embedded deeply into the schedule. Ollie commits to a five-minute meeting in Zem's office, which he has adopted as his own.

"So, how are you taking to the new job?" asks Zem, cheerily, observing Ollie's near total exhaustion and the chaos in the office.

"I am not sure if I'm the right person to lead Between Destiny," Ollie groans, slumping into the chair behind the desk.

"Of course you are."

"We have 70,000 delegates coming to Dubai, and the phone keeps ringing with SecGen wanting to know how we are going with organising it."

"It's a doddle," says Zem. "You'll be right. You know more about Between Destiny than anyone. You have been with me from the beginning. Remember how we mapped out the corporate structure and the strategic plan on the ship while we were looking for the ruthenium."

"I drew the boxes. You told me what to write in them."

"Well... You hired Erin and Cassie. And you have already demonstrated you can make life and death decisions."

"What does that mean?" asks Ollie, confused.

"The late economist, Peter Turn," says Zem.

"Yes, I remember," says Ollie, agitated. "You were hanging him out of the helicopter by the throat and I said we should let him go."

"I takes a spine to make a decision like that."

"Yeah, well, when I said 'let him go' I actually meant return to the island with him and serve him notice. You know, let him go from the organization."

"*Ahhh*," says Zem, sheepishly. "My bad, I guess."

"Yeah, your bad," says Ollie, sternly. "And you know what, Zem, I'll keep the job. I'll implement a new management style that doesn't involve performing resistance to interrogation techniques on the staff."

"*Hmmm*," says Zem, thinking it through.

"Or torture, murder or massacres."

"Well, it's your planet, Ollie. I am just a guest. And I have to go very soon." Zem looks around the office, noticing all the changes that have taken place since he was last there. There is an overburden of paperwork, and the whiteboard is a jumble of messages and diagrams hastily drawn and then crossed out.

Zem sees the big blue folder that holds the schedule. "May I?" he asks, as he picks up the document and opens the cover. The pages have green patches dotted periodically throughout.

"This green stuff is new," says Zem, breaking a smile.

"We call those meal breaks," says Ollie, with a mixture of annoyance and amusement.

"And this big one" asks Zem. "Every day?"

"That's for sleeping," says Ollie.

"Six hours?" asks Zem, disingenuously.

Zem puts down the folder and extends his hand to the tall Swede. He says, "Ollie, you are the second-best human on the planet." He shakes Ollie's hand warmly. "Get back to work."

Zem returns to the hallway. He quietly knocks on Megan's door. Eventually, she opens and Zem's light mood falls in line with hers.

Their last night together is sombre. Both are tired from the past weeks travel and shortly after a light dinner, Megan and Zem are asleep together on the bed.

Puff of Light

Zem wakes and lies, looking at the ceiling in the dark for hours while Megan sleeps beside him. These are his last minutes on Earth, and he savours the fine detail of the sensation. The scent of the air; the faint noises in the room; the warmth of Megan next to him, and the tiny, almost imperceptible movement of her body as she sleeps.

Eventually, he rises, dresses in just his pants and shirt. He collects the Transit Pouch from under the bed and leans towards Megan. He breathes in the warm scent of her neck one last time, and then stealthily exits the room. He slides the patio door quietly behind him and walks along the beach to his own courtyard. There, he pulls the dingy along the beach to the water's edge. He stoops to roll his pants up around his ankles, then steps into the boat and pushes off.

He gets halfway across the dark water to the vacant island nearby when he looks up at the Milky Way pulsing down at him. Then a very Earthly thought comes to his mind: that he will never see the Milky Way from this angle again. And this reminds him that he will never see Megan again.

He stops rowing, instantly wracked with a debilitating sense of ill ease and indecision. He looks across the dark water to Megan's apartment and thinks he sees a movement inside. Is she awake and looking for him? Has she realized that he has left? Has the pain in her chest started? Is she crying or shouting and throwing things around the room?

Zem laughs at the thought of her crazy human anger, remembering the day she fed him an egg sandwich in front of Erin and Ollie. But the laughter is a badly fitting mask for the emotional upwelling that is brewing in him. Then it erupts, like the volcano on Tanna Island, belching out great gobs of hot magma. Fluid pours from Zem's eyes, and he wipes his face with his forearm, but the pain is intense, wracking his chest and he can't row, he can't move away or towards her.

He fumbles around in the dark searching for his bag. He finds it, opens it, and reaches inside for the only thing he knows can ease the pain, the feeling that he is doing the wrong thing and the inevitability that he will not stop doing it. He tears the lid from the bottle, the very last of his Virid. He sucks it down in three long, hard swallows.

He sees a light turn on in Megan's apartment and anxiety comes over him. He puts down the bottle and strikes the oars firmly into the water and pulls, propelling the dingy towards the dark, empty island.

Megan wanders around the apartment in a state of confused sadness, she feels in her gut that Zem is receding and that it is inevitable that he will go. But this realization is one thing in her mind and another that grips her body and squeezes her. It hurts. She agreed to just let him go, but now she wants him back.

"Zem," she calls out, as she swoops around the apartment. She pulls open the door into the hallway, then the patio door and steps outside onto the beach.

In the distance, she hears a faint noise, the sound of something being dragged on wet sand, and immediately she knows what is happening. She walks hypnotically towards the water, and it touches her ankles, her calves, thighs, her belly, then she leaps forward into the sea and starts swimming. There is no anxiety about the currents or the sharks, just a rhythmic beat as her arms slice through the water.

On the island, Zem stumbles into his hollowed-out cavern. He turns on the torch and wedges it into the sand so that it illuminates the little cave. Then he strips off the last of his clothing and piles it near the foot of the steps. He retrieves the remote control on crystal meth from the bag and activates it in a way he has not done before. The lights begin to flash and pulsate. Then he replaces it in his pouch, which he grips to his chest. And then he just stands there, waiting, like a condemned man.

His face is etched with an Earth emotion called sorrow and as the seconds pass, as the milliseconds pass, the inside of the sandy cave begins to glow blue and bubbles form around him.

The bubbles become brighter, thicker, and pearlescent. They expand and occupy every square inch of the space around him.

"Bye, bye, Megan," he says, clutching the teleport pouch hard against his belly as the bubbles hum and pulsate around him.

"I love—"

CRACK!!

Zemitheree pops out of existence in a spray of bright blue light, just the way he came in.

Megan struggles from the water and runs across the sand. She reaches the top of the steps just as the final burst of blue light flashes into the night air. She stumbles down the steps to find just a pair of suit pants and a shirt on the floor and a torch, wedged in the sand, illuminating the empty cave.

She flops on the ground as a wave of emotion tackles her like a rogue wave on a surf beach. It smashes through her, pounding her sensibilities, grinding her into the sand. She feels as though she is tumbling, caught up in the violent wash and then being spat out on the beach.

And she finds herself curled up in a ball clutching the pants and shirt and staring at the circle of light projected by the torch on the ceiling.

She is breathing heavily. But she is not crying; she is too exhausted to cry. She is worn out. And above all, she is relieved that it is all over.

Six Years Later

Zem Alone

In the six years since Zem left Earth he has wandered aimlessly around the vast Parrathean ship as it moves through the Galaxy. No one has been able to connect with him, and he even rejects Music's advances, even though she knows more of what he is suffering than anyone else.

On this particular day, he finds himself standing at the counter of the teleport chamber, from where his Earth journey began. He mumbles his name to the technician behind the counter.

"Hello, Zemitheree," says the technician, brightly.

"Why did you call me?" asks Zem, gravely.

"You asked me to call you if we approached Earth's event horizon."

Zemitheree is not paying attention. He is flat and slow.

"If you know someone who wants to go to Earth," says the technician.

"Yes," says Zem, picking up. "How long will it last?"

"Not long. At the speed we are traveling, we will be past it in about thirty minutes."

"Thirty minutes?"

"Yes."

Zem's heart beats faster. He starts to speak but his words are jumbled, "Well, well... When will we be back in range?"

"We are going out wide, so probably not for sixty years or more."

"She will be gone by then," says Zem. "They don't last long, the Earthlings."

Zem moves away from the technician and sits on the plinth of the teleport machine. He has a full bottle of Virid in his hand and stares blankly at the white marble block from where he was first propelled to Earth.

Music enters the room and sees Zem sitting, looking forlorn. She notices that his Virid bottle is full.

"You haven't been drinking your Virid," she says.

"Oh, leave me alone," he moans. "I have a pain in my gut like the hunger I felt on Earth when I didn't eat."

"The Earth people call it heartache," says Music.

"It is not in my heart, it is more like in my stomach, under the diaphragm."

"It's one of their funny metaphors."

"I feel it when I think of her," says Zem, remorsefully. "I remember bits of our time together so vividly it's as if I were right there with her. And then I look around and I am alone. What is that all about Mother?" asks Zem.

Music places her fingers against his cheek and says, "I understand, my beautiful boy."

"When I smell the frangipani flower, it hurts me."

"I know this feeling Zemitheree. I have felt it too."

Zem looks up at his mother, but he can't raise a smile.

"Remember, I came to Earth a hundred years before you. We tried to stop the petroleum industry before it got strong. But we failed. In that time I found love on Earth. I know the pain you are feeling. It fades with time."

"How long will it last, Mother?" asks Zem.

"Mine has lasted over a hundred years."

"A hundred years?" he asks, astonished. "I am going to feel this way for a hundred years. There must be some way to make it stop."

"The only way is for you to be with her," says Music.

Zem looks across at the teleport technician who raises a

smile and shrugs as if to say, "What do you want to do?"

Zem puts the bottle of Virid on the ground. He takes Music's face in his hands and looks into her eyes.

"Mother," says Zem, "I will love you even if are a light year away." He places a kiss on her forehead and then steps into the teleport chamber and looks towards the technician.

By the Creek

Meanwhile, on Earth, Megan is hanging out with her brother, Al at Alligator Creek. They are resting on a blanket on the rocky outcrop overlooking the water, where it all began twelve years before. With them is a little girl aged about five. Around Megan's neck is a leather cord attached to which is the little glass vial holding the Virid powder that she stole from Zem's office on her first day on Between Island.

A radio plays a news bulletin. The news announcer says, "In New York today, representatives from Between Destiny met with the U.N. General Assembly for the 5-year review sustainable transition plan for civilization and the Living Planet."

Ollie's voice comes over the airwaves. He says, "This is a major milestone, a step towards the Verdant Age. Five years ago, we choose our destiny. And today, I can report that we are still on track."

"Chook, chook, chook, chooky," says Megan. Her little girl looks up, giggling. Megan picks up the child. "Come on honey, let's go down to the creek, and see if Daddy is back. We can tell him the news."

oOo

www.ingramcontent.com/pod-product-compliance
Lightning Source LLC
Chambersburg PA
CBHW021231250626
47155CB00008B/2961